UNDERCOVER ORC

A COZY MONSTER ROMANCE

SWEET MONSTER TREATS / MONSTERS, PI

AVA ROSS

ENCHANTED STAR PRESS

UNDERCOVER ORC

Sweet Monster Treats, Round 3

Also part of the Monsters, PI world

Copyright © 2024 Ava Ross

Editing: JA Wren and Owl Eyes Proofs & Edits

*For all my monster-loving readers.
I couldn't do this without you!*

ALSO BY AVA ROSS

Mail-Order Brides of Crakair

Brides of Driegon

Fated Mates of the Ferlaern Warriors

Fated Mates of the Xilan Warriors

Holiday with a Cu'zod Warrior

Galaxy Games

Alien Warrior Abandoned

Beastly Alien Boss

Bride of the Fae

A Sci-Fi Holiday Tail

Monsterville, USA

Monster on Board

(co-written with Alana Khan)

Love at First Orc

Monster Mate Hunt

Sweet Monster Treats

Brides of the Zuldrux Warriors

Monsters, PI

Shared Worlds:

A Monster Worth Fighting For

Mated to the Dragon

Craving Stardust

Dad Bod Dragon

Swamp Thing (You Make My Heart Sing)

Jasmine's Enchanted Genie

You can find her books on Amazon.

UNDERCOVER ORC

**She doesn't do anything spontaneous or wild
. . . until a hot orc dares her to try something new.**

Bailey: As head librarian in my small town, I take my job seriously. So when I hear a sound in the library's attic while I'm working late and alone, and then a big, green, muscular orc creeps up behind me, I smack him in the head with a stapler. After the theft of an ancient orc book on loan to the library, is it any wonder I'm skittish?

Katar explains he heard me scream and only wanted to help. He's . . . upset, and I guess I can't blame him.

He offers to help me discover who stole the book, and we track down one clue after another. But when he dares me to give into my wild side, I start falling in love.

Katar: Being hit in the head with a stapler is an interesting way to meet my fated mate. That's who this prim and proper, incredibly gorgeous librarian is. I only came to town to discover who stole the ancient orc manuscript. Then I'll return to the orc kingdom forever. But the thought of leaving this curvy, delectable woman makes me want to snarl.

So I'm going to crack this case. I'm going to show Bailey how to let loose. And then I'm claiming her as my bride.

Undercover Orc is part of the Sweet Monster Treats shared world, plus adjacent to Ava's Monsters, PI Series. It's a sweet and steamy standalone romance featuring a cinnamon roll orc with a creative . . . (cough), a light mystery, size difference, a prim librarian who sometimes *does* let loose, and plenty of humor and heat.

Be sure to explore the other titles in the collection:
  Protected by the Orc, by Honey Phillips
  Arrested by the Orc, by Michele Mills

Also check out the Monsters, PI Series

Secret Agent Gargoyle

Ice Lord Incognito

Dragon Detective

Top Secret Vampire

Ogre on Patrol

BAILEY

A bang rang out in the library's attic overhead, and my heart froze.

Someone was inside the library with me.

A short time ago, I'd released a sigh of relief, and even the pile of work waiting for me on my desk couldn't steal my joy. I'd always savored the quiet and solitude I found in this quaint brick building, where I could sit, open a book, and dive into a magical world. Or stroll through the stacks, brushing my fingertips across the book spines.

Belle's beast had nothing on this place.

Rolling ladders? We had three.

Endless collections on every topic? We had you covered.

Cozy nooks for reading? We had five on this level.

Another subtle sound echoed from above.

Swallowing hard, I rose to my stockinged feet, and crept to my door and swung it open, wincing when it creaked.

"Hello?" I croaked, my voice echoing back at me in the long hallway outside my office.

After the theft of the glorious tome on loan from the orc kingdom, I was skittish.

And angry. How dare someone break into the library and steal a book?

I waited to the count of ten, and when I didn't hear anything further from upstairs, I returned to my desk.

An hour ago, after shooing everyone out, I'd closed and locked all the doors and sunk into my big leather desk chair bequeathed to me by the prior head librarian, my beloved mentor and substitute mother, Helga Merryweather. She died a year ago, and I missed her.

Imagine, me only twenty-eight years old and the new head librarian. If Helga hadn't put in a good word for me before she passed . . . Well, I didn't want to think about that. The loss of her mattered much more than a job.

Steam swirled off the cup of Earl Grey tea I'd brewed and placed on my desk. As the sun slid away, leaving darkness peppered with a few stars behind, I sipped my tea while poring through papers. Only the floor lamp behind me cut through the shadows—and just barely at that.

Maybe I'd imagined the sound.

Peering overhead, I waited, my toes curling in my stockings.

When it was clear I must've imagined the sound, I made a note to have the janitor set some mouse traps in the attic. I returned to the pile of papers, trying to make sense of why a shoe company had sent the library an invoice.

Low footsteps rang out, and I gaped at the coffered ceiling, cringing. My mouth went dry, and fear tightened its grip on my spine.

If this was daytime and patrons were around, I'd use my most stern librarian voice to call out. No, I'd stomp up the back staircase, wrench open the door to the attic, and snarl at whoever thought they had the right to explore the upper level of the building. During daylight hours, it would be mischievous kids. Or a woman lost while trying to find the bathroom.

But after the building was locked up tight? I didn't want to imagine who it could be—not after the theft.

I pawed through my desk drawers, but I didn't carry a gun. Or a bow and arrows. Where was a switchblade when a girl needed one?

Shuffles upstairs were followed by a low thud.

Should I call 9-1-1? Of course. What was I thinking? I lifted my phone only to find I hadn't plugged it in during lunch like I'd planned, and the battery was dead.

"Leave the building," I hissed, stuffing my feet into my shoes. I rose from my chair with my purse and phone in hand. The chair squeaked, but not loudly. Spying the black metal stapler that had also belonged to my predecessor, I latched onto it, clutching it to my chest like it was a shotgun ready to fire. I tiptoed to the door and carefully turned the knob.

The door needed to be lubed, and it creaked again as I tugged it open. Holding my breath, I pinched my eyes shut and remained motionless, as if doing so would keep me from being seen.

Rapid footsteps echoed overhead.

My heart came to a shuddering halt before kicking into high gear. I bolted down the hallway toward the front of the building, wishing the back door didn't alarm when it was opened and that I could escape that way since it was closer.

Reaching the foyer, I skidded across the antique wooden floorboards that clicked and groaned beneath me. Damn old place I'd loved since I was six, and I snuck into the library after school because I dreaded going home. Helga Merryweather caught me hiding on a window seat and handed me a book, The Lion, the Witch, and the Wardrobe, book one of the Narnia Chronicles. I read it, then the next, and soon I'd devoured them all. I came to the library almost every day after that and pored through the shelves for something new. It was only natural I get my master's degree in Library Science.

Gasping and with shrieks erupting from my throat, I reached the big glass front door. I scrambled with the three locks—cursing the orc security guard who'd insisted they be installed to protect their precious book. We all knew how that turned out.

Finally, I unlocked the door. I wrenched it open and stumbled out onto the big open stone deck beyond. I nearly fell on my kitten heels while rushing down the granite stairs, and I kicked them aside to run more easily when I reached the paved walkway.

Still clutching the stapler and my purse, I scrambled out into the parking lot.

Stomps rang out nearby, followed by a few grunts, but I didn't look. I wouldn't do so until I was sitting inside my car with the doors locked. Streetlights blazed beyond the lot, but they didn't shed enough light to do more than keep me from tripping over something. Certainly not enough to make me feel safe.

As I approached my vehicle, the only one in the lot, I grabbed my key fob, grateful I'd clipped it to my purse handle and hadn't buried it inside.

Wrong time to be thinking about being buried, Bailey, I thought as I drew closer to my car. The headlights flashed as I unlocked it, and with my purse swinging from my arm, I reached out for the door handle.

A hand dropped onto my shoulder.

Shrieking, I whirled, kicked the person in the shins, and chucked the stapler at the enormous, shadowy being.

It smacked against a tall orc's forehead.

Groaning, he dropped to his knees and tumbled onto his butt.

2

KATAR

A female attacked me. A tiny—as in, the top of her head barely reaching my mid-chest—*human* female. How was that even possible? I was an orc. A warrior.

An undercover agent.

And I was sitting on my ass on the pavement, clutching my head.

I doubted a woman of her size had the ability to permanently take down an orc with my training, but she'd made a good attempt.

With a grunt, I sprung to a crouch and glared at her.

"You . . ." She stretched out her hand before snatching it back. "You . . . You're an orc!"

Good observation.

"A big, green, muscular orc," she said primly. "And I will point out, you're also a somewhat handsome orc." Her hand slapped over her mouth, speaking around it. "I didn't say that."

Straightening, I scrunched my shoulders. "Only a *somewhat* handsome orc?"

"Would you feel better if I said you were devastatingly handsome?"

"*Somewhat.*"

Her pink lips curved up but smoothed much too quickly.

"You can call me Katar," I said.

"Why would I do something as informal as that? You attacked me," she gasped out.

"And your name?"

"I don't believe—"

"Name?" I barked.

She sucked in a breath. "Bailey. Bailey Everhard."

"Katar *Dolkin*." I cocked my head in her direction. "Everhard, huh?"

"It's a distinguished name. An English surname derived from Eberhard, a name with Germanic origins meaning wild boar or brave, hardy, and strong."

"Ah." I nodded slowly.

"However, my name does not matter." After fumbling to retrieve her phone from her purse, she lifted it. "You'd better run away immediately, because I'm calling 9-1-1. They'll arrest you for your offense and throw you in jail."

Not much chance of that.

"I didn't attack you," I said. "*You* attacked *me*." I pointed to the black object lying on the pavement. "With that."

"It's a stapler." She inched closer to it in her stockinged feet. "It belonged to Helga Merryweather, and she'd be horrified to see her . . . tool used in such a way."

"I don't know who Helga Merryweather is."

With a huff, she snatched the stapler off the ground, clutching it to her chest as if she'd fling it at me again if I took even one step toward her. "I'll have you know that Helga Merryweather was the head librarian for nearly sixty years until her untimely demise, when I assumed the position." She sniffed, and for a moment, I thought she was going to cry. "She was like a mother to me." Turning the stapler this way and that in the muted light, she examined it, her pretty eyes widening. "I believe you dented it."

"I think it dented my head." I rubbed the sore spot, though I doubted I'd have more than a bruise. "Why did you hit me with it?"

"You grabbed me," she huffed. "I merely defended myself."

"I heard you scream." I waved my hand toward the building. "I was . . . passing on the sidewalk when I heard you. I, naturally, only wanted to help."

Her head tilted, and her appearance finally sunk into me.

Petite.

A few years younger than my age of thirty.

Long, lush, dark red hair that blazed like dragon fire in the streetlights.

Brown eyes with incredibly long lashes I wanted to gently stroke with the tips of my fingers. I'd remove her glasses and . . .

A curvy frame that would take my cock nicely.

Fuck. Why was my cock getting involved in this? I was working, not on the prowl for a mate.

Mate? And why had that term popped into my mind?

"I'm sorry." She lowered the stapler to her side. Biting down on her lower lip like I suddenly ached to do, she glanced toward the library. "The library's closed, and I was working. The doors were all locked, but I heard someone in the attic, moving about. I was," her lower lip trembled, and her voice dropped to a bare whisper, "frankly, I was terrified."

All thoughts of what I'd like to do with my cock fled.

"Is this your vehicle?" I snarled, waving to the car. I scanned the grounds surrounding the building but saw no movement.

Her eyes widened, and she nodded. "It's mine, yes."

"Get inside it now," I bit out, placing myself between her and the library. "I'm going into the building to look around."

In a crouch, I moved quickly and quietly across the lot and onto the walkway, taking the paved path with long strides. One leap placed me on the stone decking outside the building, and I peered past the bushes on either side, seeing nothing but park benches. Another leap, and I passed through the open front door and landed in the library's foyer. I pressed myself against the wall and listened, not hearing anything except the tick of my heart.

Bailey tiptoed into the foyer.

"What do you see?" she whispered, squinting around through her cat-eye glasses.

"I told you to wait in your car," I hissed.

"This is *my* library." She drew herself up stiffly. "As head librarian, I won't permit you to bluster your way inside the building without proper supervision."

I frowned. "Bluster?"

"Thunder, rant, boast, swagger." Her posture tightened. "You know what the word means."

"Swagger?" I winced, shaking my head. "I bet your sixty-plus-year-old woman named Helga Merryweather used terms like that."

"She was eighty-seven when she departed and yes, she was an exceedingly articulate woman. I'm honored to have known her and to take her place in the library, though I doubt I'll ever fill her illustrious role completely."

I rubbed my right horn. "Look. You said you heard sounds in the attic. I need to check it out. See if I can find the perp."

"Perp?"

"Perpetrator, offender, criminal, potential felon. I'm sure you know the word." My voice came out sarcastic, but basically, I was teasing.

And the fire flashing in her eyes and the pinkening of her pretty, freckled cheeks was my reward.

"I'm well aware of what the term means," she huffed.

"If someone's here, I'll—"

"Arrest them? I assume you mean a citizen's arrest." She lifted her phone. "Shouldn't we call 9-1-1? Although, I'll confess, my phone battery's dead, so we'll have to use yours."

"I'll look around before we place a call."

She sucked in a breath. "Very well. I do appreciate that, though I can't let you saunter through the building without me being present."

She was cute, but she didn't appear willing to listen.

"Then stay behind me," I grumbled.

When she just stared at me, I stepped closer, trying not to close my eyes while I sucked down her sweet, spicy scent. This woman was going to drive me to my knees again, though in lust this time, and I couldn't seem to do a damn thing to keep it from happening.

"Not my mate," I growled, taking her hand. Fire shot through me like I'd received an electric shock.

She *was* my mate. One kiss would confirm it, but I already knew.

What a time to find her.

"Mate?" She blinked up at me through those glasses I wanted to slide off her face. I'd kiss her closed eyelids, her sweet little chin. Her neck. I'd unbutton her blouse and let my lips trail downward to her nicely rounded breasts.

"I didn't say mate," I bit out. Fuck, fuck, fuck. What was I going to do with this information? I knew very well what my body wanted to do. Take her to the nest I hadn't prepared because I never expected to find my fated mate on the planet's surface. Claim her. Show her why she'd never find anyone better than me.

"All right, maybe you didn't say mate." She blinked again. "I could've sworn you did, however, but it hardly matters." Her gaze fell to my arm. "Why are we holding hands in the library's foyer?"

I'd entwined our fingers, latching onto her as if I never wanted to let go. I lifted our hands, marveling at how small she was when compared to me, how freckles danced across her lower arm revealed by the half-sleeve of her blouse. If I kissed each one of them, would she shiver and sigh with pleasure?

Dragging my brain back to the situation at hand, I grunted and tucked her around behind me, still keeping our fingers entwined. "Remain behind me. Don't make a sound."

After tugging her fingers away from mine, she lifted her hand to her mouth and made a zipping motion, giving me a pert nod. "On it."

"No sounds."

"Oh, yes, I do apologize. You see—"

I gently pressed my fingertip against her lips. It was that or lift her to my height, press her against the wall, and kiss her into silence, something I sensed this prim, yet strangely sexy woman might take offense to.

Leave it to me to bond with a true mate who spoke like she was born in the prior century. *Fuck.*

"No sound," I repeated.

Her eyes widening further, she nodded.

I slowly removed my finger from her plump lips, watching her. When she gave me a sheepish grin that made my heart roar like a beast coming into heat, I took her hand again and, with her behind me, started down the hall.

She crept close to my back, clinging to my shirt, releasing little huffing sounds that I bet she'd make while I drove my cock deep inside her over and over again.

At the end of the hall, we came to an office, and we stepped inside. I shut the door while taking in the decent-sized area made up of stained wood half-walls, over-flowing bookcases, and a broad, antique desk with a leather chair big enough for an orc to sit on while a petite librarian straddled his lap—naked, of course.

I needed to keep my mind—and my cock—on this investigation.

A quick sweep of the room told me we were alone.

"Why did you shut the door to my office?" she asked.

"So I can speak without being overheard. Look around. Is there anything out of place?"

When she shook her head, I opened the door, and we reentered the hall. I continued to the end and checked the back door, finding it locked on the inside. A quick scan through the window showed a back lawn bordered with high blooming bushes, well-maintained flower beds, and six park benches where people could sit and read.

Nice.

We returned to the foyer and worked our way through the rooms full of tall shelving holding books, me scanning down each row while tugging her behind me.

We paused at the empty glass case mounted on a stone pedestal.

"This is where the orc tome was secured," she said, trailing her fingertip across the surface. "They haven't determined how the . . . perp got inside the case. When I opened the library that morning six months ago, I found it gone. It's a scandal, I tell you. A horrifying incident for our well-respected library that will go down in infamy."

And that was why I'd come to Mystic Harbor. After the theft of a very special orc tome on loan from the kingdom for a year, the royal family sent me to track down the perp and bring them to justice.

For now, I wanted to remain undercover.

"I think I heard something about the theft," I said, watching her face. She wasn't involved, was she? It wouldn't be the first time a sweet, innocent looking female was the ringleader of a criminal organization.

"The police interviewed me, of course, but I was with a friend that night—"

"A man?" I barked.

She frowned. "Actually, no, my friend Vera. We went to the paint bar, and we . . ." Blinking up at me, she caught me staring. "We were painting. Having wine. But I will stress again, we were at a *paint* bar."

"I see."

"I don't drink often. I promise you, I only had one glass of wine."

"No need to explain."

"I feel I must. I wouldn't want you believing I get drunk. Ever."

"While painting?"

"That night's offering was an impressionist reimagining of Starry Night. I feel mine is a worthy copy."

"Is that right?" I had no clue what she was talking about, but I did like listening to her talk. She had a low, husky voice that contrasted with her prim wording. Plus lush pink lips I kept picturing stretching around my cock.

However, if she had an alibi for the night of the theft, she probably wasn't involved with the heist—though I wasn't ruling her out yet.

Finally, we found ourselves back in the foyer.

"How do I get to the attic?" I asked softly.

She pointed to a door at the end of the hall by the back exit and tiptoed behind me as I strode in that direction.

"Why aren't you wearing shoes?" I asked.

"I kicked my kitten heels off on the walkway. They're hard to run in."

"Then maybe you should wear practical shoes to go with your practical . . ." From the frown on her face, I sensed I was taking this convo in the wrong direction. "Demeanor," I finished lamely.

Her freckled cheeks pinkened, and she tried to tug her fingers away from mine. I held tight, liking the physical contact, though not the way my cock kept twitching about said physical contact. "I . . . I . . . I'll have you know that I let loose every now and then."

"Let *what* loose?" My damn imagination was going haywire.

"Everything," she breathed. "I'll also point out that this only happens if I've had *two* glasses—small ones, mind you—of wine."

I nodded slowly.

"Once, I . . ." She lowered her voice and peered around, clearly worried we weren't alone. "I got up on the stage and performed karaoke."

"What's that?"

"Singing along with the music to a popular song."

"What song did you sing?"

"I don't remember."

"Yeah." I frowned. "If I asked nicely, would you be willing to go to your office, lock the door, and wait there while I investigate the attic? You could sing while you're there if you want."

"No."

I suspected she'd say that.

With a twist of my lips, I opened the door and stepped onto the landing. "What's downstairs?"

"A basement."

I moved in that direction, and she flicked a switch to turn on the light before following. We reached the dirt floor, and I scanned the empty area, seeing nothing of concern.

"Back upstairs," I said, returning with her to the landing.

She promptly switched off the light.

I peered up the dingy, still-lit stairwell, though with only one bulb. "Did you leave the light on up there?"

She gasped. "I did not. That would be a colossal waste of electricity."

"Yeah." I released her hand. "Wait here." I'd barely started up the stairs before she clutched the back of my shirt and held on, climbing after me.

I huffed. "I told you to wait."

Her eyebrows lifted. "I heard you quite well, thank you very much."

"But you're ignoring my . . . suggestion."

"Are you suggesting I must only do as you tell me?"

I sighed. "I guess not."

"Very well, then. Proceed."

With a grumble, I continued to the top, pausing at the cracked open door.

"You do this?" I thumbed toward the unlocked panel.

Her eyes wide, she shook her head.

Listening, I heard nothing, but if someone was here, they would've heard us when we entered the building. I doubted we'd find much in the attic, but it would be a mistake not to check it out after the theft.

I cracked the door wider and carefully poked my head inside, scanning the tidy room with neatly stacked boxes lining the left side of the big open space. A window at the end let in streetlight, just enough to see . . .

Gasping, Bailey stabbed her finger toward the right wall.

Boxes had been dumped out and the contents were strewn all over the wide wooden floorboards.

3

BAILEY

While Katar strode around the attic, poking around the neatly stacked boxes and grunting, I stared in dismay at the papers and books lying on the floor near the right wall. Boxes had been stacked quite high there, and the contents had held a large collection. It was horrifying to see everything scattered about.

"How could someone do this?" I asked, my eyes stinging. It was silly, really, to cry about old things dumped on the floor without a care, but they belonged to the community. They were history and should be treated with respect.

Katar strode over to stand beside me, his hands on his narrow hips. When I sniffed, he awkwardly placed his arm around my shoulders and tugged me against his side.

"I'm sorry," he said. "Can you tell if anything's missing?"

"I'll have to do an inventory. I have a list on the computer in my office. Each box is carefully labeled with a number that corresponds with a document identifying its contents." I looked up at him. Gaped up at him, actually. "You're awfully big."

I felt comically small compared to him, like he could scoop me up and hold me in a way that would make feel protected. Cherished.

Sexy.

I'd given up on ever feeling sexy. If I was lucky, guys wanted a first kiss after a first date. Which wasn't a regular occurrence. My lips hadn't received any action in over a year. I guessed that proved how forgettable those first dates that didn't turn into second dates had been.

Oddly enough, I suspected I'd not only remember a first date with Katar, but also crave a second.

As for his kiss—

"As you pointed out, I'm an orc. We're all big." Wry humor came through in his voice, and when his darker green lips curled up around his tusks, I pretty much swooned.

"What's it like kissing with tusks?" The words came out before I could snatch them back, a strange occurrence for me. I was a sedate, consistent individual. I didn't take risks. I wasn't impulsive.

Yet I wanted to lean against him. Slide my fingertips across the back of his neck. Tug his head down close to mine and—

"I imagine it's the same as kissing without them." One corner of his full lips quirked even higher. "Want to give it a try and find out?"

Like I was gasoline-soaked tinder and him a lit match, I was set ablaze. "Oh, I . . . I . . ."

"Yes or no, sweetheart?"

His growly voice fanned the blaze.

"I . . ." Hold on for one second. How could I be thinking about how gorgeous he was and how much I wanted to kiss him when the library had been horribly violated? Helga Merryweather would never have found herself in a situation like this.

Helga Merryweather hadn't been matched with an orc who made her knees tremble either.

"I appreciate you being here with me," I said in a neutral voice.

"Does that mean no?"

I didn't want to say no. I wanted to say yes, yes, yes. A thousand times *yes*. How did women let a guy know she was attracted to him?

"Raincheck?" I blurted out.

"Explain."

"It's a rather old term, originating in baseball in the 1800s. Spectators who attended games that were postponed or cancelled because of weather could receive a ticket to attend a future event. Thus, in this situation, it means perhaps not now but perhaps in the . . ."

Crap. Could I please stop talking?

As I spoke, his smile grew, and a devilish glint darkened his eyes. "Will I have to wait for it to rain to collect that kiss?"

"Perhaps just gusty weather."

Damn, I was flirting. Also something Helga Merryweather would never have done. For the first time, I realized my substitute mother had been a bit . . . stodgy. Reclusive.

As well as unkissed. She'd never married, and she told me once she was happy that she hadn't.

I'd mirrored my life after hers, but did I want to leave kissing this orc out of the equation?

I swallowed and tried to drag my mind back to the present. Kisses could wait for wind gusts. "I'd be terrified if I were facing this alone."

"As you said, you could call 9-1-1 once you'd plugged in your phone. The cops would come immediately."

"I should still call them. Notify them of this latest incident." I frowned. "Do you think they'll question me as extensively as they did after the theft of the orc manuscript? I was exhausted by the time they were finished."

"You told them the truth."

Why was he looking at me with vague suspicion?

"Of course I did. I held nothing back." I drew myself up stiffly and made myself back out from underneath his warm, muscular arm. "I didn't steal the book, and I didn't do this."

"Never said you did."

I deflated as quickly as I'd puffed up. "I'm sorry. I'm stressed. Overwhelmed by what happened six months ago, let alone now. Why would someone do something like this?"

"I assume they're connected."

"But how? We had one orc tome and nothing else of any value. Yes, we have first editions within the library, but they're not books someone couldn't pick up on eBay if they looked hard enough."

"That's what we're going to find out."

We? I liked that.

"Let's note the numbers on your boxes," he said. "And then we can go look at your inventory." He tipped his head toward the stairs. "Perhaps we can discover a clue when we know exactly what we're dealing with." He paused at the opening to the stairwell and took my hand again, his hooded gaze meeting mine. Flames swirled there.

Was he overheated?

"And after that ..."

I held my breath.

He flashed me a tusky grin. "And then we can go outside and see if it's gusty."

4

KATAR

I loved teasing Bailey. Talking with her.

And I was praying the wind had picked up outside.

With me leading the way, we took the stairs to the ground level. But when we entered her office, we found it in shambles.

Bailey collapsed against the wall, rocking a floor lamp when she inadvertently brushed against it.

I straightened the lamp and scooped her up in my arms. I wanted to take her to her car and lock her inside while I looked into this, but I got the idea she'd refuse to leave me. And frankly, I wanted her where I could keep my protective eyes on her at all times. I settled for lowering her gently into her desk chair and wheeling it back away from the rubble.

"Someone . . ." She gaped up at me, her finger sweeping across the mess. "We were only in the attic for a few minutes."

I should've locked the front door. No, locked Bailey in her car and then searched the place alone.

"I'm so sorry." Irritation churned through me, combined with the need to keep her safe.

"I don't understand why anyone would do something like this. Do you think they were searching for something?"

It had to be connected to the theft of the book.

"Where do you keep that inventory?" I asked, sensing what she'd soon tell me.

Her trembling finger shifted to the desk. "It's on my . . . Oh, my gosh. My laptop is gone. Gone . . ." When she cupped her face, I stooped down in front of her, taking her chilly hands in mine, warming them. I kissed her knuckles, and she looked at me with teary eyes. "Someone destroyed my office." She took in the papers scattered all over, the books flung from the shelves, lying in ungainly piles on the floor.

If they were only looking for her laptop, they would've taken it and fled. "What else did you keep here? Anything of value?"

She shrugged and when a tear trickled down her cheek, I wanted to find whoever did this and rip off their head. I settled for stroking the tear from her face with the pad of my thumb.

"We'll figure this out," I said. "I promise."

"Again, I'm so glad you're here." A sob shook her frame. I tugged her from the chair and into my arms, dropping down onto the floor with my back against her desk. I should lock all the doors and search the place from top to bottom, yet everything important was nestled in my arms.

"I'm not going anywhere," I said gruffly. "I promise this as well. I'm here for you for as long as you need me."

"Thank you." She shuddered and looked up at me, and her pretty eyes stunned me all over again. So did her silky hair I kept fisting at the nape of her neck. And the way she molded her body against mine as if she belonged there.

"Did you feel that?" I croaked.

Her lips twitching, she shook her head. "No. What do you mean?"

"I felt a gust of wind."

Just like I thought, her lips curled up sweetly, which was my goal when I said it. "Now you're trying to cheer me up, make me feel less afraid. I appreciate it."

"Maybe I also want that kiss."

"Then what are you waiting for, Katar Dolkin?"

All I could see were her lips parting and the way her gaze locked on my mouth.

I feathered my lips across hers, tender at first, not wanting to hurt her. She was so much smaller than me. Infinitely precious.

And incredibly responsive.

She moaned and turned to wrap her legs around me, her fingers digging into my upper arms as she shifted her pelvis against me. With a gasp, she pulled away. Her fingers left my arm only to trace across her lips.

"Tusks," she said softly and with wonder. "I thought they'd be hard, but my lips fit between them. They only pressed into my cheeks."

I frowned. "They didn't hurt you, did they?"

She shrugged. "I didn't feel them. I was too . . ." Her eyes closed but only for a heartbeat. "I was too lost in your kiss. You kiss well, Katar Dolkin."

"So do you, Bailey Everhard." I wanted more. So much more. But now wasn't the time.

I shifted her off my lap and back into her chair, rising to stand over her. I wanted to wrap myself around her, shield her from everything and anyone who might be a threat, but I really needed to make sure we were alone inside the building.

I said as such.

She scrambled to her feet, leaning against my side. "I'll come with you while you look."

"I still can't convince you to wait in the car or here, behind a locked door?"

"I'm terribly sorry, but no."

Because she was stubborn, I wanted to growl and gnash my teeth. But I also liked having her with me where I could watch over her.

We went to the front door, finding it wide open, and shut and locked it. Then we covered the entire first floor and scoped out the basement and attic again, finding no one inside the building.

"I should call the police now," she said in a tiny voice once I'd sat in her office chair and tugged her onto my lap. She leaned back against me sweetly.

"Go ahead. I'll stay with you."

"Thank you." She plugged in her phone and made the call.

We waited until a police officer arrived and let him

inside, explaining everything that had happened. He took a bunch of pictures with his phone before grunting and studying us.

"And who are you?" Detective Carter asked, his tight gaze raking down my frame.

"An orc who was passing by on the street," I said carefully. It would be easy to pull out my badge from the orc kingdom, but I was told to be discreet. The kingdom hadn't notified the human authorities I would be here. I could work quicker and quieter without all the fanfare that might come from an official state visit. "I heard Bailey cry out and ran to help her."

She slunk closer to me, taking my hand. "I would've been terrified if he wasn't here."

"Do you have any ID?" he asked.

I pulled it out and handed it to him. It was a simple thing with just my first name and picture, but it also indicated I was here on a diplomatic mission to aid in ongoing treaty negotiations. Orcs had emerged from the ground years ago and integrated with human society. We were treated like visitors from another country, not the monsters a few people shouted when they first saw us. When it came down to it, we were people like everyone else.

Orcs bought homes, took jobs, and dated humans. Most had accepted us as part of their everyday lives.

Detective Carter studied my ID longer than necessary, but it had been produced by the kingdom itself, and he wouldn't find anything suspicious there. With a grunt, he handed it back and watched me as I carefully returned it to my back pocket.

He sighed and directed his attention to Bailey. "You need to close the library for the rest of the week while we investigate."

Not a bad idea.

"I can't," she gasped. "We have activities planned. Three sessions of reading hour tomorrow and Thursday for differing age groups. The local romance book club is meeting here tomorrow evening at seven to talk about their latest read."

"Romance club?" I asked, curious.

"They're reading an orc romance." She winked. "It's called Candy for My Orc Boss, and it's steamy."

"Steamy?" Detective Carter frowned. "People actually write books about orcs?"

"Romance books. Well, I assume other genres as well, but orc romances are hot right now."

His brow creased.

"This one features an orc male and a woman." Bailey grabbed a book off the floor beside her desk and handed it to him.

I leaned over to study the cartoon orc on the cover, plus the woman holding a lollipop. She was looking at the orc as if she wished she was holding—and about to lick—*him* instead.

My low laugh rang out. I loved it.

"Have you read it?" I asked.

"Yes, I facilitate the romance book club."

Perfect.

The detective huffed. Bailey shared her frown with both me and then him. "It's a fun book. Sweet. Romantic. Steamy, as I said."

"I don't discount that orcs and humans can . . ." The detective coughed. "Back to the subject at hand, if you please."

"Yes. As I said, the romance book club needs to meet here tomorrow night. You know the coffee shop is closed for renovations, which means they can't meet there. And the reading groups and the book club aren't the only ones using the library this week. Did you know many of the elderly come here not only for books but for regular socialization? And children come here after school. It's spring and while not too cold outside, there are times when children have no secure place to go until their parents get home from work."

"I quite agree," someone said sternly.

We turned to find a middle-aged man standing in the open doorway of her office. He gasped as he took in the disarray. "My goodness, Bailey. What happened here?"

Bailey explained about hearing a sound in the attic, running outside, and us searching—leaving out the impact to my forehead with the stapler, which the man now held.

"How horrifying. You poor dear." The man placed the stapler on the desk and held out his arms.

Bailey hesitated but went to him.

Seeing another male holding her made my guts churn, but I swallowed down the bitter taste in my mouth. I'd just met her. She didn't belong to me. Even if she *was* my fated mate, something I'd verified with our kiss. No matter what, she was still her own person.

But it was all I could do not to snarl.

"How did you know?" she asked him.

"I heard the call on the scanner."

"Ah, I see. Katar." She returned to my side and waved toward the other male. "This is Flynn Jacobs. He's the chairman of the board overseeing the library. Flynn, Katar Dolkin was here when I needed him most."

"You should've called me immediately," Flynn said curtly, though his eyes held concern. "I would've come right away."

Was there something between them? The hug suggested yes. My growling belly shouted there better not be.

"There was no need." Bailey leaned into my side. Did she realize she'd gravitated back to me instead of the man who was acting as if he had some say in how she ran her life? "Katar was here."

I took her hand and gave him a proud grin. While my chest shouldn't puff from the fact that she'd chosen me over him—sort of—it still did.

He blinked a moment, his attention falling to our clasped hands before he stiffened. The look he sent me did not contain the warmth it had when he gazed at Bailey.

In fact, I had no problem reading the sharpness there.

My jawline tightened.

Challenge accepted.

5

BAILEY

"Well, I'm here now," Flynn said, his brow narrowing on Katar. "You, sir, can leave. I'll take care of Bailey and help her handle this horrifying incident."

Detective Carter looked between Flynn and Katar, though I wasn't sure why his lips were compressing. "I'm going to take a look around."

"Can I tidy up here?" she asked.

"Anything missing?"

"My laptop."

He grunted. "I guess you can straighten things out. Keep a list of whatever's missing." He strode from the room and his footsteps echoed in the hall and then on the stairs.

"I'll help Bailey," Katar said pleasantly, his fingers tightening on mine.

Flynn and I had dated over a year ago, but we'd mutually agreed it wasn't working out. I'd even heard he was seeing someone new. So why was he scowling at Katar and glaring at our clasped hands? Despite one steamy kiss I itched to repeat, Katar and I were only friends. Acquaintances, actually. We'd only met a few hours ago.

I shrugged off the feeling Flynn was acting proprietary. I was upset and couldn't be reading him right.

"It's late. You should go," I told Flynn. "I'll remain here until the detective is finished."

"I don't mind staying to . . ." His glare deepened as he took in Katar. "Make sure you're okay."

"I am. Really. You can go." I flicked my hand toward him. "As Katar said, he'll stay with me."

"All night if she needs me." His voice was a low rumble that made my heart do spontaneous things like dance the mambo.

"You're sure?" Flynn held out his hand. In the past, I would've taken it, and he'd hold me. While our relationship hadn't worked out, we'd remained friends.

With the situation at the library, I needed all the friends I could get.

Disengaging from Katar, I stepped forward and took Flynn's hand. He tugged me into the crook of his arm and urged me out of the office and down the hall.

"Are you *completely* sure you're alright?" He shot a glare over his shoulder and leaned toward me, lowering his voice. "If you're . . . in trouble. You know. The theft or *anything* at all, you can trust me to stand with you and help you through it."

A peek told me Katar had remained inside my office.

"I'm fine." In the past, I'd enjoyed his kind touch. His kisses? Not much, which was part of the reason we'd called it quits. He did nothing for me, and when I confessed, he admitted he felt the same.

We reached the front door, and I tugged it open. Flynn had his own key, as did all the six board members, including our volunteers Vera and Carole. My next-door neighbor, Carole, moved to town a few years ago, buying and completely restoring the old colonial home on the other side of my fence.

"Thank you for coming when you heard the call on the scanner," I said.

He stroked my cheek. "You know I'm always here for you, even if we're no longer together. The theft of the book was enough, but this! Well, the book may be gone, and may I say, I'm sure someone has added it to their private collection already, and I doubt we'll ever hear about it again, but you and I are a team. There isn't much I wouldn't do for you."

We hadn't exactly been together; it was only a few dates, but I nodded. He was still a good friend, and there were times when a woman needed all of those she could get.

"Call me tomorrow," he said, his hand dropping to his side. "Let me know what the detective finds out."

"I will."

I watched as he strode down the walkway and got into his car parked next to mine in the lot. After he'd pulled out onto the street and drove away, I closed and locked the front door.

Back in my office, I sighed.

Then I got to work, picking everything up and placing

it in tidy piles on my desk. Katar helped, periodically shooting me concerned looks.

"You're sure you're alright?" he rumbled.

"I'll be fine." Eventually. My body shook, and I wanted to go home and curl up on my couch.

After I'd finished organizing things and taking an inventory, I called one of our volunteers, Vera. She often dog-sat for me if I needed to be out of town or would be gone too long for my doggie's elderly bladder. Like always, she'd use the spare key I hid in my backyard.

"Hey, I'm working late. Could you let Mozzie out?" I asked. Mozzie was short for Mozzarella Sticks, my pup's name.

"Of course. If I can drag your potato off the couch," Vera said with a laugh.

A geriatric fox terrier-poodle-plus everything else tiny mix, Mozzie did enjoy snoozing.

"I really appreciate it. I'll let him back in when I get there."

"Working late again?" Two years older than my twenty-eight, Vera was single like me. She was on the prowl for a husband, however—unlike me.

My gaze shot to Katar, who was gently lifting books and carefully placing them back on the shelves. Few people treasured books like me, but it appeared Katar did.

"Yes, late." I'd tell her about the break-in tomorrow. She worked as an accountant in town and volunteered in the library.

"I'll give Mozzie some treats when I'm there," Vera said.

"I owe you."

"I'll call it due the next time I go away. You can sit with Puff." Her very social mixed Siamese cat who didn't like to be left alone for more than a few hours.

"It's a deal." I hung up and slumped in my office chair while Katar finished returning the books to the shelves. "Thanks for doing that."

"No problem. You have some amazing books." He turned and leaned against the wall next to the floor-to-ceiling bookcase, scrolling through one of the books. "This is a first edition of Charlotte's Web."

"Helga Merryweather gave that to me six years ago on my birthday. After she adopted me, she gave me a book each year, all first editions."

"That was nice of her."

"She had her lawyer mail me this year's present after she died, but I haven't opened it yet." I wasn't sure I could. It would hurt terribly, reminding me that the woman I'd called Mother was gone forever.

"When's your birthday?"

"In a few weeks. She wasn't just my boss here at the library. She essentially raised me because . . ." My face overheating with embarrassment, I looked down at my hands wringing on my lap. "My parents had a problem with drugs. When they overdosed when I was fourteen, she went to the courthouse and got permission to raise me." I'd called her mother and gave her chocolates each Mother's Day.

"She sounds like an amazing woman."

"She was." I smiled as memories washed over me, soothing me. "She loved to bake, and we made cakes and cookies all the time. We didn't eat them—well, not all of them." My rueful laugh rang out. "We donated many of our creations to the homeless shelter in town. Anyway. Every night, even though I was old enough to do so myself, she'd read to me. That's where my love of books came from. She died a year ago." I traced my fingertip along the book's spine. "Helga was sweet, seamlessly stepping into my parents' place. She'd wrapped each book in special paper, and I opened them on my birthday." After this birthday, however, there would be no more gifts from her to open.

"I'm sorry you lost her, that your parents weren't there for you when you needed them." He carefully placed the book on the shelf.

"Thanks."

"I feel like I want to hug you again," he rasped, staring down at me with warmth in his eyes. "But if you're not the kind who enjoys things like that, let me know."

He must've seen me shrug away from Flynn. With Katar, however, it already felt different.

That kiss . . . I couldn't stop thinking about it and how I'd like to do it again. It hadn't felt like mashing mouths together like with Flynn. No, it felt like losing a part of myself but then being put back together in a new and different way.

"I like hugs," I said softly.

He pulled me into his arms and held me. No hands roaming where they shouldn't—a common thing with guys who said they wanted to give you a hug but were really just looking for an opportunity to grope. No caging me against the wall to turn this sexual, also something too common with guys I'd met through dating apps.

When the detective walked into the office, we pulled apart. I swore I felt us sever, as if strands of warmth had connected us but were suddenly sliced through in a messy way.

Odd, but the feeling must come from the connection I felt with Katar already.

"I didn't find anything suspicious," the detective said, his sharp gaze looking back and forth between us. "I took pictures in the attic." He scratched the back of his neck, his gaze shooting between us. "We can save the questions for tomorrow if you'd like."

"Thank you. I'm exhausted."

He gave me a slow nod.

"Do you think this is connected to the theft of the orc tome?" I asked.

"Hard to say when that happened six months ago, but we won't dismiss the idea."

I wasn't sure I had much information to offer, but I set up a time to speak with him in the morning, here at the library.

As he left, I gathered my things including my purse I'd tucked into my right desk drawer when we were tidying. There was no evidence that the person who'd ransacked my office had tried to break the lock. Maybe they weren't searching for money. Which begged the question. What *were* they looking for?

"It seems silly to lock up when someone's already been inside," I said as we stood on the deck, and I turned the key in the front door. I was already mentally reorganizing my morning to accommodate the detective's visit.

"Can I give you my number?" Katar asked as we walked to my car.

I handed over my phone, and he typed it in.

"I'll be happy to help you in the morning," he said as I slid into the driver's seat.

"You don't have to do anything like that."

"I'm a diplomat, but we don't have anything planned for the next week. Let me help you?"

He pleaded so sweetly, I couldn't say no.

Actually, I didn't want to say no. I wanted to see him again, even if it was only to organize everything in the attic.

"I appreciate the offer. I'll be limited for time, but at eleven, one of our volunteers, Vera, will arrive to take over the desk. I'm free until two, when she has to leave."

"Perfect." He rested his hand on the open doorframe. "I can be here when you meet with the detective as well. I'm essentially another witness."

"Good point. Would you like to come by the library before nine, then?"

He nodded, and he leaned toward me. For a moment, I thought he'd kiss me again, and my heart flipped over at the thought. But he straightened and frowned as if deep in thought before backing out of the opening.

"Tomorrow," he said.

With a nod, I shut the door and started my vehicle.

It didn't take long to reach my small home. I left the car in the driveway rather than lift the garage door to put it inside. The door opened hard, and it was one more thing on my list that needed fixing.

Helga Merryweather had left me the tiny, two-bedroom cottage her dad built. Despite it being a home-made, campy thing with stuff always breaking, I treasured the security I'd found there from the time she took me in. I'd moved into the cottage after she died and tried to piece my life back together again for the second time.

My salary at the library was decent, and owning a home helped with my monthly expenses, but there never seemed to be enough for all that needed to be done.

I entered through the breezeway connecting the single-vehicle garage to the small house, kicking off the kitten heels I'd retrieved. A soft woof from my left told me Mozzie was done with his nighttime adventure in our backyard.

But when I went to unlock the door leading from the breezeway into the house, I found it cracked open.

My fingers froze on the knob. I never left it like this. After watching my parents be robbed almost monthly for whatever stash they might have hidden, I was hyper about security. Vera was just as vigilant. She would never have left my home unlocked.

Chills rippled across my skin.

Someone had been inside my home.

Were they still here?

6

KATAR

I'd just dropped onto the king-sized bed inside my hotel room when my phone buzzed. Thinking it was someone with questions related to my case, I swiped into the call and barked. "Lo?"

Jerky breathing came through the line. Prank call?

Irritation burned through my gut. "Yeah, well—"

"Katar," Bailey shrieked. She lowered her voice. "Katar?"

Not liking how panicked she sounded, I bolted upright.

"Bailey," I said, my training kicking in. I slipped my footwear back on and was halfway to the door before she finished speaking.

"Someone was inside my house! They may still be here!"

The shrill yip of an animal punctuated her words.

"Give me your address," I said. "I'm on my way."

"Please." I could almost see her sagging. "I appreciate it so much."

"Where are you now?"

"Inside my car in my driveway. The doors are locked."

The harsh yips continued. "What's that sound?"

"Mozzarella Sticks."

I frowned as I tugged the hotel door shut and started across the parking lot. "Excuse me?"

"He's Mozzie for short. My dog."

"Ah, yes." I'd only seen dogs on the streets but never interacted with them. We had different sorts of pets in the orc kingdom.

She gave me an address, and I punched it into my phone, the GPS showing me I was only about a half a mile from her place.

"Stay on the line," I said as I broke into a run.

"What sort of vehicle are you driving?"

"None. I'm running."

"Why?"

"Because I don't need a vehicle."

"You don't even sound winded," she said breathlessly.

"I run a lot." And work out a lot. It came with the job. And I was breathing fast already, though not from my efforts. My heart was thumping like the drums of Urbone during the fall festival. While orcs danced and spun, the drum's pace would accelerate until the dancers feverishly thrashed.

I was terrified about what might be happening with Bailey.

"How long will it take you to get here?" she squeaked.

"Five minutes or so."

"You're close." Relief came through in her voice and the barking had stopped. "Thank you."

"Any time." Always.

I rounded a corner and sprinted the rest of the way, seeing a vehicle sitting in the driveway running, its parking lights on.

"I'm here." I slowed when I reached her drive and walked the rest of the way up to her vehicle's side door.

She cracked the window and squinted up at me. "I'm so glad you're here. I was scared."

The fear in her voice made me gnash my tusks. I wanted to track down whoever had terrified her and bash their head in. A primal thought, but that's how it was with mates.

I wouldn't tell her about that—yet. We'd only met today.

But before I was finished with this assignment, I'd make sure she not only knew she was mine, but that she agreed we belonged together forever.

"I'm going inside." I studied the tidy home in sore need of repair. The roof needed replacing, and I'd repaint the exterior, though it was clear someone had done it within the past few years. It wasn't perfect, however, and it would be once I was finished with it. Her front gardens were lovely; she'd had work done there or done it herself. But I would really make it shine.

Well, I'd do all that with her permission, of course. While she was mine in my mind, she hadn't yet agreed.

She would.

"I'll go with you." She unlocked her car door and opened it, holding a light tan dog in her arms. "This is Mozzie." She held up the pup for him to sniff my hand.

While I didn't know dogs, I, like all orcs, adored pets.

Mozzie's gray-flecked brow tightened as he delicately sniffed my fingers. Then he started wiggling. It was all Bailey could do to hold him. His spiked tail twitched, and he whined.

"I think he likes you," she said with a nervous laugh.

I held out my arms, and she stepped into them with her pup between us.

Mozzie continued to squirm, trying to reach my chin with his tongue.

"He doesn't usually like strangers," she said in a hollow voice. She shook, and I wanted to blast whoever had scared her. "But he must sense you're a good person."

"I like to think so. Glad your dog agrees."

Her lips curled up on one side before smoothing. "They say animals are good judges of people—and orcs, too, I suppose." She stepped away from me. Mozzie squirmed and whined, still straining toward me.

I pulled the blade I wore at my waist.

"Whoa." Bailey blinked at it, her eyes widening. "That's some knife."

Frowning, I held it up. "Doesn't everyone carry something like this?"

"I never have, but I'm beginning to think I should." Turning, she rounded her car and entered her garage with me following.

"Is anything out of place?" I took in the three-tiered shelving spanning the back part of the building holding plastic boxes with labels and neat writing.

"Not that I can see. There's nothing out here but holiday decorations, outdoor games, and boxes holding my outside furniture cushions. A few other odds and ends. Nothing of great value." She climbed two steps to a door on the right, opening it and gesturing for me to enter ahead of her. "The breezeway door was unlocked, as is the one to my house, and I'm diligent about locking everything. But the door to my backyard was unlocked when I got home and partway open. Vera came by earlier to let Mozzie into the backyard, but she's as strict about locking up as me."

"She has a key?"

She pushed her glasses up further on her nose. "It's hidden in the backyard. Only a few people know about it."

I nodded slowly as I walked through a tidy entry area with a mat holding boots and sneakers, plus pegs with jackets and a thick coat, and stopped at the entrance to the main part of her house. "Why don't you wait in the car?" I didn't have much hope she'd listen when she hadn't at the library, and I suspected we were about to see a repeat of what we'd discovered in her office. "I want to make sure there's no one inside. You'll be safer in your car. Mozzie too." I added the last as an incentive. She may be willing to endanger herself, but I could already tell that she was fiercely protective of her pet.

"While I agree with you on principle, I'm going with you. Mozzie will sound the alarm if there's someone inside."

I stepped into a neat dining room adjacent to the kitchen, where the countertops were empty other than a jug of cooking implements next to the stove, a vase with a bouquet of flowers at the head of the island, and a bowl holding apples, pears, and bananas to the left of the sink.

Other than a medium-sized dining room table with four chairs, there was a hutch holding pottery and delicate china and a sideboard with a few decanters in the dining area.

Mozzie peered around but didn't bark, a good sign.

Bailey closed the door and put him on the floor. He scooted into the kitchen and over to a placemat holding bowls of water and dog food and proceeded to nibble, looking at us as he chewed.

"He's a great watchdog despite his size," she said. "That tells me no one's here." She swallowed. "No one appears to have touched anything in these rooms." Her gaze shot to the hallway to the right of the kitchen. "My bedroom's through there. There are stairs on the right in the hall that lead to the open loft. That's where I slept when I lived here with Helga."

I strode to the kitchen and tucked aside the curtain over the glass panel in the back door, studying the small deck outside and the fenced-in yard beyond, but seeing no movement. After, I scooted up the stairs to the small loft, noting she used it as storage now as there was no furniture. Returning to the first level, I ducked my head into the tidy bathroom across from the door to the loft, before crossing the dining room and peering through the arched opening, taking in a living area across the way.

A growl rumbled in my chest. If only I could shield her from this.

She hovered behind me, clinging to the back of my shirt.

Mozzie trotted up beside me but stopped in the

entrance, a low rumble rising in his throat. His fur bristled, and his tail spiked out.

Bailey gasped and rushed past me.

I scooped my arm around her waist, holding her back. "Let me go first."

She looked up at me, nodding, and tears trickled down her cheeks. "Why would anyone do this? Why?"

I took in the complete devastation. Someone had not only flipped the furniture; they'd dumped the bookshelves covering the left wall onto the floor.

"Do you have any idea what someone's searching for?" I asked.

7

BAILEY

"I don't get it. I don't have anything of much value. Helga didn't either." My voice croaked, and I slumped against the living room archway, staring in horror at the mess someone had made of my things. "Helga left me this house and a little bit of money. It's not enough to do more than basic maintenance, and, well, librarians rarely get wealthy from their wages. My point is, I don't own anything worth stealing. A few pieces of jewelry, perhaps." My gaze shot toward my bedroom. Was that also in shambles? "But they wouldn't fetch much at a pawnshop."

He strode through the rubble to my bedroom doorway.

I almost hated to look. Following him, I took in my bedding strewn on the floor, my bureau drawers emptied out, the jewelry box from Helga open on the top of the bureau, and the closet door open and everything inside disheveled, obviously sorted through.

"We need to call the police," he said.

With a nod, I did so, and they said they'd send a detective right away. Mystic Harbor was a small seaside town with three thousand and twenty-two people. I was sure Detective Carter would soon make a prompt appearance. What would he think of the latest installment in my life? Pure shame filled me. Helga Merryweather would never have allowed anything like this to happen.

"Anything missing here?" he asked.

"Should I look around before the detective arrives?"

He shrugged. "You can look. Just don't touch anything until he's taken pictures."

I snooped first in the living room, and Katar stood in the doorway, watching, his knife still in his hand.

I gestured to the blade. "You might want to put that away before he gets here."

As he slid it into the sheath at his waist, I tiptoed around the sofa and past the piles of books. "For some reason, I feel less violated in this room. I *sleep* in my bedroom. Knowing someone went through my things, touched my bedding." I sighed. "Knowing they were in that room feels more . . . intimate, I suppose." Utterly devastating.

Someone knocked on the front door, and I opened it, letting Detective Carter inside.

While Mozzie yipped and went over to sniff his shoes, he stood on the mat, his sharp gaze scanning the living room. Finally, he nodded and lifted his phone. Without commenting, he went around the room, taking photos, then moved to my bedroom. Mozzie followed, his tail wagging as if he and the detective were old friends.

I stood in the open doorway, cringing as he snapped

pics of my lacy underwear flounced on the floor, my high thread count sheets stretched out like Mozzie had gotten a hold of them and run, and my skimpy nighties draped on nearly every surface. The intimate parts of my life should not be on display, even for those hired by our community to protect us.

"Anywhere else?" he asked, stopping beside me.

I swiped the tears from my eyes and shrugged. "Everything upstairs looked normal, didn't it?" I asked Katar, and he nodded.

"Come with me, then." Detective Carter entered my bathroom, and I hovered in the doorway. A few things appeared to have been shifted on the sink, but otherwise, the room looked untouched.

He opened the door to the loft and peered back at me. "You can wait here if you'd like."

"I don't keep much up there. Old clothing. A few things of Helga's. I store everything else in the garage."

With a nod, he climbed the stairs, returning a few moments later. "Looks untouched."

I sagged back against Katar; grateful he was here. How had I gone from being a strong, independent woman to someone who clung to a guy I'd only met today?

He'd fit seamlessly into my life already.

"Have you had a chance to inventory your things?" the detective asked.

"No," I said in a tiny voice.

Katar's arms tightened around me. Mozzie trotted over and sat, looking up at me and whining. My little friend sensed my distress and wanted to give me comfort.

I picked him up, and he settled easily in my arms, looking between me, Katar, and Detective Carter.

"If you could take a look and let me know tomorrow, I'd appreciate it," the detective said kindly. "Someone's obviously looking for something and they think you've got it. We need to know if they found it or . . ."

Or if they'd follow me until they obtained whatever they were seeking.

After making a bunch of notes and taking more pictures, he left.

With Katar's help, I straightened the sofa and put my board games, puzzles, and books back on the shelves. After picking everything up in the bedroom, though we tossed everything in bags to be washed, I sunk onto the couch and tried not to cry. Mozzie hopped up beside me and laid his head on my thigh, looking up at me with mournful eyes.

"What's happening to my easy life?" I asked the room in general. "I feel like it flipped over or I was sucked into an alternate reality. I'm a librarian. I own this house, but I barely get by. I don't have wealth. I don't own precious antiques. What do they want?"

Katar sat beside me and tugged me up onto his lap, holding me.

"I don't know," he growled. "But I'm going to find out."

8

KATAR

"I'll stay with you tonight," I said. There was no way I'd be able to sleep at my hotel while she remained here alone except for her dog. And I doubted the hotel allowed pets.

Bailey shifted in my arms. "Oh, I couldn't ask you to do anything like that."

"It's not a bother at all. I want to help you, and this seems to be the only way I can do it." I glanced at the piece of furniture we sat on. "I can sleep here or on the floor."

"You're a big guy. Take my bed. It's a king. I . . ." She frowned.

"You what?"

Her face pinkened. So adorable. I wanted to kiss her cheeks. Feel the warmth there with my mouth. "I optimistically thought I'd someday share it with someone."

She was my mate. I wanted to behave like my ancestors. I'd track down the threat and eliminate it. Return to her and strip off our clothing. Beat my chest while roaring.

Then claim her body until she'd come so many times, she would only want me.

I doubted she'd want to share her bed with me, so I didn't offer. But the thought of being with her in that way or even just having the chance to hold her through the night made my cock shoot toward the sky. It shoved against my pants, wanting out.

Or inside her.

"Maybe one day," I said. "You'll share it with someone."

She blinked up at me through her glasses, and one look from her sultry eyes was all it took. I gently slid her glasses off and laid them on the table in front of the sofa. Then I stared into her eyes unimpeded, still marveling at the fact that she was my mate. Already, my heart was softening, opening to only this female. It wouldn't take much effort on her part to make me fall so hard and fast I wouldn't remember wanting anyone but her.

"You're staring at me," she whispered.

"Did you feel the wind?"

A frown took over her pretty face. "The doors are shut. The ceiling fan isn't running."

"It's gusty in here. You must agree."

The quirky smile she gave me sliced right through my chest, leaving me gasping. "Now that you mention it, I do feel a bit of wind. What should we do about that?"

I didn't need any further invitation. Leaning close, I closed my eyes and drank in her sweet, spicy scent, savoring how it flamed through my veins, setting wherever it touched ablaze.

I kissed her. Plundered her mouth. Claimed her in the way of my people, in the way only an orc could do.

Her lips parted, and I delved inside, my tongue teasing across hers.

She moaned, clutching my shoulders, clinging as if the heat flaring through me had transmitted itself to her.

Shifting around, I laid her beneath me on the sofa, bracing my palms on either side of her shoulders while I continued kissing her.

I was already lost in this woman. I'd never find myself again unless I was with her. Part of this was the growing mate bond, but the rest was pure Bailey.

Heat flashed through me, making me feel as if I could conquer the world when all I really wanted to conquer was *her*.

It wouldn't take long before I'd need her so much it would consume me. Both of us if she was an orc. How did mate bonds act on a human?

Teasing my fingertips across her jaw, I moved my hand lower, sliding my knuckles across the silky flesh of her throat. As I stroked above her breasts, she moaned and latched onto my horns. She was so touchable, so responsive.

As her fingertips ran up and down my horns, shockwaves blasted to my cock, stiffening it further. Did she know that horns were erogenous zones, that a male could come if a female rubbed them enough?

Her ankles hooked on my ass, and she rocked her pelvis against my hard cock, each grind of her body shooting me higher into the sky. I was so lost in her; I didn't care if I ever found my way back. With her, I'd finally found a home.

I lifted my head and looked down at her. I took in her beauty, the way her pupils had contracted, the black disappearing from her eyes. The gold flecks had multiplied, and they blazed with the heat reflected in me.

Her hips stilled, but her fingers kept gliding along my horns.

"If you keep doing that, I'm going to explode," I said.

"Doing what?"

"Grip my horns tighter. Rub them. And then you'll find out."

"I don't know much about orcs. I've never touched horns before."

"I'm eternally grateful to hear that."

Her head tilted, and she studied my face. "Are you saying my stroking them is turning you on?"

"I'm saying that you stroking them is going to make my cock blast against the inside of my pants."

"Oh." She sucked in the word. "That's . . . intriguing."

"Orcs have lots of cum."

"Lots of cum," she echoed. Then her fingers stilled, and her eyes widened. "Rubbing your horns is like rubbing your cock."

"In some ways."

I watched her thick swallow go down her throat.

"Do you want to come?" she asked.

I groaned. "What a tricky question."

A smile flitted across her lips that were plump and ripe from my kiss.

She tugged her hands away, though it appeared she did so reluctantly. "You probably don't want all that wetness inside your pants."

"I'd sacrifice my pants."

"If you're going to stay here, you'll need other clothing then." Her lips quivered, and her eyes gleamed with a hint of lust. "Then, if what you're wearing gets . . . wet, you'll have something else to change into. Because . . ."

"Because what?"

"Because I thoroughly enjoy stroking your horns."

Fuck. My sweet, prim librarian had a sultry side I hadn't expected.

A primal roar rose in my throat, but I bit it back.

"Are you suggesting that you might be interested in touching more than my horns?"

A full smile took over her face. "You did point out that it's windy."

9

BAILEY

I'd only kissed Katar twice, and I was ready to drag him off to my bed. Find out exactly how much cum he could produce. Okay, I also wanted to keep stroking his horns. It was empowering to think I could turn him on with such a simple touch.

I'd never been one to give into my sexy side. Even when I had sex, something I hadn't done since one botched attempt with a man I dated before Flynn, it wasn't fun. The man came almost immediately. After groaning and rolling off me, he went to sleep while I lay there wondering exactly why I'd bothered. I hadn't even been fully worked up, or I would've taken care of it myself.

I had a feeling if I slipped between the sheets with Katar, I wouldn't be lying there after wondering what I'd missed out on.

I slid out of his arms and when he sat up looking all flustered and kissable, I stood between his thighs while he cupped my hips in his big, brawny hands. "I propose we share the bed."

His breath jerked in. "Exactly what will that entail?"

"For now, sleeping. As tantalizing as your cum and stroking your horns is," they were SO tantalizing, "I feel like we're rushing this. We only met today. I only know your name, that you're a diplomat from the orc kingdom, and that . . ."

His head tilted, and he watched my face with complete fascination. "And what?"

"That I want you despite barely knowing you."

He groaned and scrubbed his face with his palms. "You're killing me here, Bailey."

"That's not my intention. I just think we need to slow this down a bit." Even if he was staying here with me.

"I can do that."

What would my neighbors think of a male staying at my house? Helga would snort and tell me to go for it, but she'd been . . . freer than me. She'd gotten staider in her later years, as she noted to me, but she once shared that she'd been a true flower child, even going to Woodstock. She'd planned to marry someone, but he was killed in action overseas. I saw pictures of him—them together—and it was clear they were in love. It was very sad that she'd lost him.

When I was still a teenager, I'd dreamed of having something like that for myself.

Silly me for transferring my dream relationship onto Katar. For all I knew, he was married, or—

My brain screeched to a halt, and I blurted out the words. "You're not married, are you?"

He leaned away from me, and for a second, I thought it was a rejection, that he was married, and he was about to tell me. But he lifted me as if I didn't weigh more than a toddler and plunked me on his lap, wrapping his arms around me. "I'm not married. I'm not in a relationship with anyone. There's only you."

My breath caught. "Only me?"

"There will only *ever* be you."

Whoa.

He tilted my chin, making my gaze meet his. "Did you think I could kiss you like that, hold you like this, if I was with someone else?"

I shrugged. "Some guys do."

"I'm not some guys."

I was quickly realizing that.

"You're the only one I want in my life." He nodded as if he'd come to a decision deep inside. "When an orc meets his fated mate, the person the fates crafted just for them, they know."

"How do they know?"

"At first kiss, it's like sparks of heat blasting through them, centering in their . . ." His lips curled up on one side. "Well, in that area you seem to want to get wet."

"You're saying it's cock related."

"My cock is only one small part of it. It's a feeling that consumes every bit of the orc. Wonder. Lust, sure. A need to protect and be with that person all the time. That's you, Bailey. You."

"You felt . . . sparks when we kissed?"

"I did."

"I'm not sure what to think of all this."

"Which is why I'll try to take it slowly."

"Try." That one word dominated his statement.

He shrugged. "I'm an orc with a strong sex drive. Trying's all you're going to get out of me, sweetheart."

And maybe my sex drive had taken a sudden bolt in a new direction. I'd always felt there was a side of myself I hadn't unlocked. That Bailey would take what she wanted.

She was wild.

Did I dare let her loose on Katar?

He lifted me—and I was no lightweight—and placed me an arm's length away, then rose, towering over me. "In this, you're right. I also think we should wait at least a few days before taking this further."

My rocketing pulse suggested it was going to be torturous to wait even that long, but I was a principled woman. I didn't rush into *anything*.

"Come with me to my hotel to get my things?" His flinty gaze scanned my small living room, and I suspected if a threat suddenly appeared, he'd rip it apart to protect me.

"See? I didn't even know you were staying in a hotel."

"There's no embassy nearby."

"And yet you're working on a treaty. Why stay in tiny Mystic Harbor?"

His gaze swept across the room again. "We do the work remotely. I've got a computer."

I hadn't really thought about what kind of tech orcs might use. "You have internet in the orc kingdom?"

He shrugged. "Doesn't everyone? We didn't for a very long time. Orcs were slow to adopt the technology humans consider vital for living. But when we decided to emerge from our lands far below the ground, we knew we'd have to adapt. We initially worked with your government to obtain what we needed to catch up, and honestly, most orcs can't imagine not having phones or computers now. I'd say we're about equal to your country as far as tech goes."

"I understand working remotely. A lot of people do that. But why did you pick Mystic Harbor in particular?"

"Why not?" His level gaze held mine, but for some odd reason, I suspected he wasn't telling me everything. That was okay. We all had secrets. Well, most people did. I wasn't sure there was anything about me and my life that everyone in town didn't already know, some of it quite embarrassing.

"Sure, why not?" I said breezily. "And sure, I'll go with you to your hotel." The thought of remaining here alone, even with Mozzie's dubious doggie protection, made shivers erupt deep inside me.

"I don't want to leave you alone for even one second," he said. "But I ran here."

I frowned. "That's right."

"If I remain on the surface, I plan to get a truck."

Orcs didn't fit well inside small cars, and those who drove bought full-sized pickups or even the trucks used to haul big boxes on the highway.

"We can take my car. No need to run back to your hotel." I scanned his frame. "It'll be a tight fit." I tilted my head. "I'm sure running's great exercise, but it's dark out. Where are you staying?"

He named a hotel I was vaguely familiar with. "That's at least three miles from here."

"A short jog."

I marveled at how fit he was, how his muscles rippled beneath his clothing when he moved, and how he always seemed tight and poised to respond quickly to any threat. If I didn't know better, I'd think he was some kind of orc secret service agent. CIA. Whatever the equivalent was in the orc kingdom.

But someone like that wouldn't hang out in Mystic Harbor, let alone give spontaneous protection to the town's librarian.

"If you're looking for a run, I won't interfere, but you're welcome to ride in my car." Though I doubted anyone would bother me in my car even if I was alone.

He paused before releasing a grunt. "Very well. I'll ride with you."

Sensing action, Mozzie jumped off the recliner and came over to sit beside me, his spiky tail snapping against the wooden floorboards.

"What do you think, Moz?" I asked. "Should we go with Katar to get his things?" I met Katar's gaze, liking the warmth I found there. "You should bring back enough for tonight and tomorrow, and we'll reevaluate this after we speak with the detective. He may have leads already, and this horrifying incident could be over within a day." Though I suspected it wouldn't be.

After strapping Mozzie into his harness and attaching his leash, I grabbed my keys and purse, and we locked the house and went to my car I'd bought with my own money three years ago. A hybrid, I was quite proud of it. I'd been putting a little extra on it each month and it would be paid off by the end of the year.

But it was like a kiddie car when compared to Katar.

I buckled Mozzie into the backseat, and he whined, used to riding up front. Spoiled pup. But Katar was not going to ride in the back—or inside the trunk.

He opened the passenger door and studied the interior.

I trotted over, easing around him to slide the seat back as far as it would go, smiling while waving my hand. "In you go."

"Yeah." With a sigh, he placed one foot inside and settled in the seat, his body curling forward to keep from hitting his head on the roof. Even with the seat back, his knees scrunched against the dash. It was like trying to stuff a giant into a tiny cardboard box.

"Are you okay?" I asked, trying not to laugh at the pained expression on his face.

He looked up at me, his eyes sparkling with humor. "I'm okay. Just . . . get there fast, would you?"

"You should buckle."

"I'm not sure I could get it around me at the moment."

I nodded slowly. "It's important to wear a seat belt."

"I get that, but . . ." Another sigh, and he dragged the belt forward and wrangled it across his tight abs, somehow securing the end in the clasp.

"Good job." I realized I must sound like a prim schoolteacher about to award a good boy a sticker and laughed again.

He huffed as if he thought the same thing and shot

me a smirk. "I'm not always this well behaved. You should know that."

My blood started humming. "I usually am." Why was I still hovering in the car door opening?

"*Usually*?" His thick brow ridge lifting, he peered up at me.

"I think . . ." OMG, I was going to take the plunge, wasn't I? I lifted my chin and met his gaze with a challenge. "I believe I'm ready to give in to my wild side."

10

KATAR

To say our ride to my hotel was uncomfortable was an understatement. Mozzie whined. Bailey gnawed on her lower lip, squinting through the windshield. I tried to ignore the cramps building in my thighs.

And her lovely scent. When an orc found his fated mate, he felt more stable when he was around her, when he could scent her.

Or lick her, but that was taking things in a direction she seemed to want to hold off on. And I agreed . . . mostly.

"Wild side?" I asked, crooking my neck to watch her as she drove.

My cock had kicked into high gear when she made her statement. While I floundered, she shut the door and placidly walked around the hood of her car to get inside beside me.

I'd sat there, stunned, while my cock tried to find a way to rise in this twisted position.

"I've always felt there was a part of me I didn't . . . let

go, I guess you could say. Like something brewed within me and under the right circumstances, it would break free and go crazy."

"I see," I croaked. "Actually, I'm not sure I do. Explain."

"I've lived a life of restraint. I'm not a psychiatrist, but naturally, I've analyzed myself."

"Naturally."

"We have many books in the library on how the human psyche impacts our everyday existence. I grew up in a world full of turmoil. My parents were high most of the time or sleeping it off. By the time I was seven, I knew how to cook my own ramen, prepare a lunch, and get to the bus stop on time. Alarm clocks can be tricky things, but I figured it out."

It crushed me that she'd lived like that. And it made me mad that her parents hadn't been there for her, that she'd had to raise herself.

"They weren't meant to be together. If they'd been sober enough, I'm sure they would've gotten a divorce. They snarled at each other all the time, and our home was a parade of men and women stopping by to buy drugs or get high with them."

"No one . . ." I hated even bringing it up.

"I got very good at hiding. The park's a wonderful place all year round. You can sit on the swings and if a mom is there with her kids, you can kind of stay near her and creeps don't realize you're alone. The library was even better," she breathed. "Helga welcomed me every time I poked my head inside the front door. Often, she'd have a book waiting for me and sometimes, a drink and a snack. She'd sit me down in a quiet alcove where I was within her sight, and she'd periodically smile at me. I felt safe, perhaps for the first time in my life."

"I'm grateful you had Helga." I'd kiss the elderly female if she was here, and I was sad I wouldn't get to meet her.

"But to answer your unspoken question, no. No one was able to come near enough to do something like that. And I got out of the situation before it became an issue."

"By moving in with Helga."

"Such a relief when she stomped into the child protection agency. They took me there when my parents were found and had started to talk about foster care. She insisted she'd take me and within a year, she adopted me." She turned onto the road with my hotel. Mozzie was silent. He'd put his front legs up on the side of the door and was looking out, his head darting back and forth from us to the view. "She was amazing. I'm not sure what would've happened to me if I hadn't had her in my life."

I hated that Bailey had to grow up that way, that there hadn't been anyone there for her until an elderly librarian intervened.

She brought the vehicle to a stop at a light and waited for it to turn green before driving forward. "I believe, from my studies, that it's normal for someone experiencing a childhood like mine to take control of whatever they can. I translated that into controlling every aspect of my life, including my sexuality. I restrained it. Hid it, I guess you'd say, like I hid myself from my parent's turmoil."

"No child should have to live that way."

She turned into the hotel lot and followed my pointed direction to my unit. "Many do, sadly. I've thought of fostering a child myself, but I'd have to fix up the loft first. Going to live with Helga helped. She was sweet and kind. She showed me what a normal life could be like, but I still held onto the reins of whatever I could. As I said, it was completely natural. I'm sure I'm not the only kid in the world who's done something like this."

"I'm sorry."

"It's messed up, right?" she said with a low laugh, shooting me a rueful look. "I didn't share all that for pity. I wanted you to know why I act the way I do and why I might now want to change. With you . . ."

"Me?" I held my breath, waiting to hear what she'd say.

"I want to let go, to be the person I might've been if my parents hadn't done drugs, if they'd been there for me like they should've been. If I'd had more than a few library couples as examples of how relationships should work."

"I hope you can find that person inside."

The hotel was made up of units with parking in front. She drove into the spot I indicated, shut the vehicle off, and stared toward the dark room ahead.

"I think I can . . ." She turned to face me. "This is going to sound completely wild," her jittery laugh burst out, "there's that word again. Wild. But it fits. This sounds like I'm out of my mind . . . *Wild* is much better. Wild!"

She bit down on her plump lower lip again. I wanted to run my tongue across it, soothe it. Okay, not soothe it. Nibble on it myself, then take my nibbles down across her body. Her gaze met mine, and I couldn't figure out what the flecks of gold shining there might mean. They were like brilliant stars swirling together. But I sensed a change in her that was reflected in her eyes. As if she'd come to a big decision and was going to make an announcement.

I nodded, encouraging her to continue.

"I want to go wild with you, Katar, but I have no idea how to do it. Would you teach me?"

11

BAILEY

He said nothing for a very long time. Years, it felt like.

At least a minute.

Then his tongue—long and thick—darted out to run across his upper lip. His tusks.

"I've made you uncomfortable," I finally said.

"If you could see my cock trying to stand at attention among my scrunched-up limbs, you'd know exactly how uncomfortable I truly am."

I frowned. "Are you saying my request has turned you on?"

"You're my fated mate. Just being near you turns me on."

My low laugh came out different from any before. It sounded . . . husky. Sexy. As if I was aroused. Which I was. His simple words made heat shoot through me, centering in my core. I was getting wet without direct stimulation, something else that had never happened to me before.

"You don't need to say yes," I added.

"Oh, I'm saying yes. I'd be wild and out of my mind myself if I told you no." He twisted, somehow bringing his knees around to rest on the console between the seats, facing me fully. "Explain exactly what you want from me, sweetheart, because I'm going to give it to you any way I can."

My heart floundering, I sucked in a breath. "Wild, for me, isn't all about sex. Just putting that out there."

"We did say we wanted to wait at least a few days before taking things in that direction."

"That seems about right."

He grinned. "And in between then, I assume you want me to teach you how to let go, to be the person you've kept locked inside all your life?"

"It sounds crazy when you put it like that."

"I accept."

I lifted my eyebrows. "Are you sure?"

"I'm moving in with you anyway, right?"

"That was to be with me until we figure out why someone broke into my office and home, plus see if we can determine what they're searching for. You're staying with me to make sure they face justice."

"I'm staying with you to protect you. To hold you. To tell you that you're gorgeous and that there's nothing I want more than to taste every single bit of your body."

Whoa. I was going to melt onto the floorboards. "I, um, sure."

He flashed me a tusk-filled grin, and I remembered how our mouths fit together, how his tusks weren't hard and that they didn't hurt. My mouth fit in between them, and his lips . . . They were full and made my skin tingle wherever they touched.

"I'll be happy to teach you how to go wild," he said. "Orcs are good at stuff like that."

My laugh snorted out. "I know so little about orcs."

"You, with all those books at your disposal?"

"You know we don't have much about orcs there. You guys are new to humans. I mean, there are some fiction books featuring orcs, and the romances, but in most of them, orcs are snarly beasts in fantasy stories. They eat children and use the finger bones to pick their teeth."

He placed his palm on his chest. "I promise I don't eat children."

I tilted my head. "What *do* you eat?"

"Everything humans do. We have our own delicacies, but most are consumed within the orc kingdom. We're slowly bringing them to the surface with mixed reviews. You know what it's like. Some human cultures eat insects, yet others cringe at the thought. We have our own specialties we love that others might find unusual or cringeworthy, but I'm happy to say most people are willing to give them a try."

"I want to try some of your favorite dishes."

"I'm an excellent cook. I think we can call eating orc dishes as part of your lessons in going wild."

"Excellent."

"Let me go get my things—*all* of my things?" At my nod, he continued. "I'll check out of the hotel, and we'll return to your home."

Mozzie yipped as if in agreement.

"I'll wait here with him," I said.

He grew stern. "Keep the doors locked and hit the horn if you see or hear anything suspicious."

My nod jerked out.

He pried himself out of my car and waited until I'd clicked the locks before entering his hotel room. He didn't take long, and I popped the trunk for him to put his things inside after. Once he was back in his seat, I drove across town, parking in my driveway. Nothing appeared changed at my house, and I breathed a sigh of relief once we were back inside and the doors and windows were locked, and I noted everything looked the same.

We did some more tidying, and I was happy once my world felt like it was returning to order again.

"First lesson," he said after he'd placed his bag inside my bedroom and returned to the living room.

Sitting on the sofa, I tilted my head, looking up at him. "What's that?"

"Take off all your clothing."

I gulped, but *hell, no* didn't roar up my throat. Actually, my body went suddenly languid, and if he touched me down there, he'd find me slick with desire.

Smiling, I rose from the sofa, moving to stand close enough to him I could pick up his scent. Cinnamon? Like, give me all the hot crossed buns right now, you cinnamon roll hero.

"What are we going to do once we're naked?" I whispered.

"Strip, sweetheart, and you'll find out."

12

KATAR

"When fated mates meet," I said, "it's orc tradition for the couple to remove all their clothing for an assessment."

"I can understand wanting to check things out before going farther."

"And to taste if things go as they should."

Bailey sucked in a breath, but I didn't find reservation on her face. Just an openness that called to the wild side inside me. She wasn't the only one who restrained herself to feel in control. "I can . . . handle that."

"I'm a bastard," I blurted out.

"What does that have to do with removing our clothing?"

"My parents weren't mated. I don't even know who my father is. Just putting that out there."

"With my history, you must know I don't care about your background except for how it impacts you today. I want to hear whatever you're willing to share. I . . ." She paused as if in thought and slowly nodded. "I want to hold you when you're sad and do fun things for you to cheer you up. Funny how I feel that already."

It was the mate bond. Once fated mates met, a hormone was released inside them that drove them to quickly crave each other, to fall in love fast. Were my mating hormones working on her? No one knew if they'd activate the same feelings inside humans all the time, though there were couples proving it worked here on the surface already.

"My mother's the orc king's sister," I added. "She died but never told me who my father is."

"I'm so sorry."

"Sometimes, I don't care. Other times, I wish I knew. It might be interesting to meet him if he was willing. The rest of the time, I just try to forget."

"I understand wanting to put sad things behind you." She tilted her head. "Does that make you a prince?"

"Not really. There are plenty of orcs ahead of me in line for the throne. My parents weren't true mates. They were only together a few times. See, he met his true mate and told my mother it was over. She . . . neglected to tell him she was pregnant with me." I scratched the back of my neck. "I don't know how I'd feel if I met him. It's hard to feel anything for someone who was never a true parent."

"I understand."

"It's not his fault, I suppose, if he never knew I existed."

"Wouldn't he guess?"

I shrugged. "If he has, he hasn't approached me.

Maybe he lives far from the central city. As for my role, I'm pretty much an employee of the orc kingdom."

"A diplomat, you said."

"Yeah . . ." I scrambled my fingers through my hair. "About that."

"You're not a diplomat?"

"I feel that I need to be honest about everything before we go wild."

Her laugh snorted out. "I'm all for honesty."

"You shared so much with me that was painful for you." I held her upper arms, staring down at her, hoping she could see how earnest I was about this. I wanted her to know everything, and I hoped she wouldn't reject me once she heard it all. "I'm not a diplomat in the true sense. Yes, I'm working on a paltry part of the treaty, but I was sent here for another reason, one your government is unaware of."

Her eyes widened. "Nothing illegal, I hope."

"Nothing that would break your laws or ours."

"Then what's the big secret?"

"Some might say me being the bastard is enough."

Lifting one eyebrow, she tapped her foot on the floor.

"I'm undercover," I blurted out.

"Ah, so you're like . . . an orc cop?"

"I'm a secret weapon of the orc kingdom. I was sent here to figure out what happened with the orc book and do anything necessary to get it back."

"*Anything*." She frowned. "You mean like kill someone to obtain it?"

"I'll do my best to avoid that."

"Whoa. You're like an orc . . . James Bond."

I cocked my head. "Never heard of him."

"He's a fictitious secret agent. He can kill people with simple, everyday objects like a pen or . . ."

"A stapler?"

Her smile made my heart jump around and booteliers flutter in my belly. I grinned right back at her.

"Yeah, a stapler, and I apologize for hitting you with it."

I shrugged. "It didn't kill me. But as for your James Bund—"

"Bond." She deepened her voice. "James. James Bond. We'll have to watch some of the movies."

"Movies featuring a fictitious character?"

"Oh, to most of us, he's one hundred percent real. He's gorgeous and sexy and . . ." When I grumbled, jealous when I shouldn't be, her smile widened. "He's nowhere near as gorgeous or sexy as you, however."

"You, my mate," I tugged her into my arms, "are utterly perfect. You're also gorgeous and incredibly sexy." Already, my warm feelings for her were transforming into something deeper, something lasting. I couldn't imagine not seeing her all the time, not being with her. That was how it was for fated mates, and I could only pray to the fates that she'd travel this path with me.

"I'm not your James Bond," I said.

"That's probably a good thing, since people are always trying to kill him."

"I doubt anyone would kill me to obtain an ancient orc text."

"Do you think the break-in at my house and the attic is connected?"

"That's what we're going to find out."

"How?"

Good question. "There has to be a connection, and we'll find it."

"And in between then." She stepped out of my embrace and slid the hem of her blouse up across her gorgeous body. "We'll get naked and go wild."

13

———

BAILEY

I'd only turned on one small lamp, and it didn't generate much light. I wasn't too self-conscious about my figure, but despite Katar's kind words, did anyone think they were perfect?

"I'm trying to figure out what we're going to do once we're naked," I said. After removing my glasses and setting them on a table, tugged my blouse up over my head and tossed it onto the sofa. I was trying to let go, feel free. And ignore my skin peppering with goosebumps that had nothing to do with the temperature.

Mozzie sat nearby, looking back and forth between us as if he wasn't sure if we were going to put on PJs and go to bed or do something . . .

Okay, we were going to go *wild*.

"Have you come up with any conclusions?" Katar's smoldering eyes locked on my breasts covered in a lacy bra, and he seemed to stop breathing. His hand lifted toward them but stopped before touching.

Should I lean forward until we connected? While I

knew it took friction to make nipples harden, mine hadn't gotten the text. They pebbled and throbbed. So did my clit, for that matter.

"Maybe we'll raid the neighbor's vegetable garden."

"Anything good there?"

"Zucchinis are tasty."

"They're big."

My gaze centered on the big bulge between his legs. "Why yes, they are."

"We're not raiding zucchinis." His tongue dipped out to touch his upper lip before he snatched his hand back and unbuttoned his shirt, shrugging it off.

"Will we streak to the center of town and paint something nasty on the road with spray paint?"

His head tilted, and he frowned. "Would you really do something like that?"

"Honestly? No. I'm in enough trouble with Detective Carter already. Can you imagine me trying to look some of the library patrons in the eye if the local newspaper did an expose on the librarian's latest antics?"

"Latest implies you've done something like that before."

"First, then."

"No streaking or painting."

"I have to admit, that's a relief."

"Yeah."

"You mentioned tasting." Feeling brazen and with my head swimming as if I was drunk, I unhooked my bra. I hadn't had any alcohol, but Katar was going straight to my head.

"I did." A flick of his fingers undid the fastener on his

jeans that so nicely hugged his muscular thighs. And his butt, something I couldn't help but notice whenever he turned around.

And the big bulge below his zipper—that was shifting.

Feeling a touch giddy, I slid my bra off and tossed it on top of my blouse.

Was I really going to do this?

Yeah . . .

Katar groaned, and his bulge grew bigger behind the fabric of his pants. Was I going to get to see it all tonight? To taste it? I wanted to glide my tongue along his rocky jawline, trail it down his neck, see if his pecs tasted as amazing as they looked.

His abs. Muscles rippled beneath his green skin as he splayed the fabric of his jeans wide.

"Naked, sweetheart," he rasped, his pupils so blown his eyes were completely black.

I shimmied out of my panties and straightened in front of him, my skin prickling from the cool air, nervousness, and the thrill of anticipation. "Your turn."

"You . . . You . . ." His eyes glided down my body like a caress, and shivers tracked through me. I wasn't cold, but he was incredibly hot. I worried he'd burn me with one touch.

Was I a fool to strip for a guy I just met today?

Probably.

Maybe.

I didn't know!

It just felt right, so I was going to go with it.

He yanked his jeans down and kicked them aside,

standing in front of me wearing absolutely nothing but a devilish grin.

"Now what?" I asked with a quiver of excitement.

He strode forward, swept me off my feet and strode toward my back door. "Now we go wild."

14

KATAR

While the only thing I wanted to do was lay Bailey in the grass and get on with the tasting, orc mating rituals had to be respected.

Out in her fenced backyard, I paused in the grass to look up. The stars overhead would witness this event much like the tiny glowing insects coating the cavern rooftops did back in the underground orc kingdom. To think that there was so much more to this world than the mysterious caverns far below, that up here, there were such vast heavens watching us, protecting us.

She hugged her arms around her chest.

"None of that," I said, taking her hands and squeezing them.

"We're naked."

"I'm very much enjoying the view." I slid my gaze down to her breasts, taking in her pink, puckered nipples, then traced my eyes across her lush belly to her thighs I ached to part. She had sunset-colored hair between her legs, another difference between orcs and humans since our only hair was on our heads. I wanted to touch it, find out if it was silky or some other texture. I'd part the strands and seek her clit, the wetness between her thighs I knew would be waiting.

"You've got a hard-on." Her attention was locked on my cock.

"Because I want you."

Her head tilted. "Do you want me because you like me or because I'm your orc mate? We haven't known each other long."

"You've made me laugh, made me feel incredibly protective, and you've given me a reason to build a new future."

"That really isn't answering my question."

"It's complicated."

She huffed. "That's what guys always say when you probe them about emotions." Her voice went gruff and growly. "It's complicated, babe."

"I'll never call you babe."

"Good thing. It's damn creepy."

"What about sweetheart?"

"Normally, I'd say it was creepy too, but when you use the nickname, it makes flames lick through me."

"A good sign." My smile dropped. I wanted to be serious. "We don't know each other well. You've pointed that out. Which is why we've given ourselves time to see where this goes. But I like you. Very much." I was already falling in love with her, as was the norm for an orc who'd met their fated one, but I sensed I'd spook her if I told her that. Maybe after a few days, she'd be open to the notion.

"I like you a lot," she said.

"Same, sweetheart. Same. That's why we're naked."

Her lips curled up. "Did someone mention tasting?"

With a groan, I tugged her flush against me. Kissing her now wasn't part of this orc mating tradition, but I couldn't help it.

I claimed her mouth, slanting mine across hers, pressing hard while stroking her lips with my tongue, demanding entrance. Demanding everything I craved, including her body, her heart, and her soul.

She gripped my arms tightly, and a moan worked its way up from her chest. Her lips parted, and I slid my tongue across hers, touching her everywhere.

Mozzie barked inside the house. We'd made him remain inside. But the sound made us burst apart, both of us grinning.

"Tasting," she said, tracing her fingertip across her lips. "We had to get naked to kiss?"

"No, sweetheart, we had to get naked to dance."

"Like . . . sway our hips to the lack of music?"

"I hear it, don't you?"

Her head tilted. "Just a cat howling at the moon a few houses down, cars out on the main road, and . . ." She frowned. "I guess I hear the tall grass in the field beyond my lawn swaying. The seed pods on the top are shifting together. Is that what you mean?"

I tightened my arms around her, determined not to let go. "Close your eyes."

Her eyelids fluttered before slipping down, her lashes brushing her cheeks. "Now what?"

"You put aside the cat, the cars, and even the seed pods and you listen."

We said nothing for a long while.

"What am I supposed to hear?" she asked, a touch of exasperation coming through in her voice.

"Can you hear the stars whispering? The orc kingdom, as you know, is located deep beneath the ground. We have no stars, no moon, no sun."

"Is it cold down there? Dark all the time?"

"Neither. The roofs of our caverns are covered with tiny insects that generate light. They find energy in the very air around them. They're our stars, and during what we call day, they blaze brightly. As their power fades and while they regenerate, their lights dim, and we call that night."

"It sounds incredible. Is it pretty?"

"As lovely as your stars, only different."

"But there's no music in that."

"Oh, there is. Keep listening. I can hear your stars whispering just as I hear the insects when I'm home."

"The bugs are probably rubbing their legs together or something like that."

"Listen."

She paused. "Maybe I hear something."

"You'll feel it in your bones, and it's music, the prettiest sound you'll ever hear. Even the moon creates its own tune. If you listen hard enough, you'll hear that too."

"It's more like a whoosh, not a true melody."

"It's a subtle sound we can dance to. Keep your eyes closed." I lifted her into my arms and swayed to the music I heard not just with my ears but in my heart. Only those falling in true love could hear it, and it blazed across my soul because I was with Bailey.

"I love being held by you. Love that you're swaying around my backyard. Love that we're naked."

"When you remove all the trappings of today, you can sink into the person you'd be no matter where and when you might live. You're not Bailey, the librarian—"

"*Stuffy* librarian who is proper and staid."

"Never that," I vowed. "That's not how I see you. You have magic in your soul. You just haven't learned how to let it out."

"How do I do that?" she groaned in frustration. "I think I hear the moon and the stars, but when I open my eyes, I'm sure I'll see that the sound I'm hearing is insects in the grass and maybe the swish of a rabbit hopping along a trail in the nearby woods."

"Close off the Bailey of now and listen to the one deep inside you."

I lowered her to her feet but held onto her hands, guiding her to move with the music swirling around us.

Wonder filled her pretty features. "I hear something. I *feel* something."

"Let it free. That's the Bailey you long to be."

"Ah," she sighed. "I feel it *all*." Her eyes opened, and the heat shining there made my lungs come to a halt.

Only when I was with this woman would I be able to breathe.

She gave me a sweet smile. "Now that we've danced, can we get to more of that tasting?"

15

BAILEY

Listening to the stars and the moon and dancing to the music I could just barely hear made something wild and wonderful rise inside me. And maybe that feeling came solely from being with Katar, though I wasn't going to doubt anything. He said it was music, and I wanted to believe.

He lifted me into his arms again, but when I thought he'd go inside, perhaps put me on the sofa or lay me on my bed, he dropped instead onto the grass.

It was cool and damp, but it felt heavenly against my overheated body. I was wrapped up in Katar, and there was no place I'd rather be. Was this coming at me too fast? Maybe. But I suspected if I didn't grab onto it and let it take me where it willed, I'd never find the me I'd always ached to be.

He kissed me, and I soon lost track of the stars, the moon, and even the damp grass beneath me. All I could do was *feel*. His tongue tracing along mine, his tusks pressing against my cheeks in a way that delighted me.

His fingertips glided up and down my sides.

We weren't going to take this all the way; we'd made that clear. But I suspected whatever we did tonight was going to change my life forever and drive me feral. Did staid Bailey dare to let go?

Katar's mouth left mine, and he kissed his way across my jaw to my neck, sliding his mouth back to my ear. When he nibbled on my earlobe, I groaned and bucked my hips up toward him.

Yes, Bailey was going to fully let go, and she was going to enjoy it.

Too many times in the past, an evening with a guy would turn sour. He'd kiss me a few times, touch me without any skill, and then tell me he didn't understand why I wasn't turned on. He'd get impatient.

Katar had barely touched me, and I'd turned into a raging inferno.

"You're my mate," he growled against the overheated skin of my neck. "I only want you. Need you." His fingertips, so gentle, slid to my breast, and when he cupped it, I barked out a cry.

A dog a few doors down started howling.

My snicker slipped out before it dissolved into a moan. He was rolling my nipple between his thumb and finger and what could be better than that? Oh, I soon found out when he replaced his hand with his mouth.

He coiled his tongue around my nipple, tugging. His other hand made sure my second breast wasn't feeling neglected, and he stroked the nipple, bringing it to a needy peak. While I whimpered and jerked my chest up to his touch, his fingers left my breast to trail across my belly. Under any other circumstances, I'd wince. I mean, I needed to lose weight. But Katar didn't seem to notice or maybe orcs enjoyed a lusher figure. For whatever reason, I didn't feel like sliding out from underneath him.

No, my thighs parted.

He slid his fingertips through my curls. "You're beautiful," he said against my breasts. "Are you wet for me, sweetheart?"

Very much so. I jerked my head in a nod, then closed my eyes. The stars and the moon's music hummed across my bones. Or maybe that was Katar. He'd left my breast and was kissing across my belly, stroking it with his tongue as if he'd never get enough of my taste or the feel of my skin against his mouth.

He paused, his gaze meeting mine, and I surrendered. Just like that, I was willing to give anything, sacrifice *anything* just to be with this male for the rest of my days. Was this what he meant by the fusion of two souls, the mate bond of his people? I wasn't an orc, but that didn't mean I wouldn't be affected by whatever chemicals were raging through him. Like pheromones, they'd sink into me and make me crave him for a lifetime and beyond.

"You're mine," he whispered against my flesh.

Completely mesmerized, all I could do was nod. Because he was right. I was his from the moment we met.

He continued kissing downward. When he spread my legs wider, he kissed first the inside of one thigh, then the other. Sparks flew from my nipple he stroked with his fingers to my very core, and I wasn't sure I could stand it.

But I had more inside me to give. More to take from him.

My pussy caught fire as he nudged his knee between mine.

His tongue slid from my opening to the top, where he paused. "Such a cute little bud." He shot me a tusk-filled grin. "What will happen if I taste it, if I suck on it? Will my pretty little mate get wet? Will my pretty little mate come from my touch?"

His words made me go wild. I writhed beneath him, craving it all. Craving *him*.

His tongue delved inside me while his fingers rolled my clit. He growled out his satisfaction, speaking in a jumble while his tongue flicked inside me. "You. Taste. Amazing. I'm going to eat you every day for breakfast, lunch, and dinner. I'll never need to eat anything but you again."

"You'll starve," I snorted out, grabbing onto his horns, keeping his head where I needed him most.

"Never," he vowed, though it came out like *wawa*.

His nose dragged through my curls, and he looked up at me, somehow still speaking while his tongue continued to pump deep inside me. "You smell amazing. I'm going to smell your sweetness every day of my life."

A guy who wanted to go down on me daily? Sign me up right now.

I wiggled, wanting more, and he obliged as if I'd cried out my need, moving his mouth through my wet folds. His infernal tongue kept teasing inside, where I throbbed. An ache built inside me, and soon I was going to explode and shoot all the way to the stars. *Then* I'd hear them singing for sure.

As he shifted his face back and forth, his tusks grazed

across my flesh, dragging through my wetness to the point it must coat his entire face.

He growled and nibbled, his tongue still driving deep inside me. I was being fucked by a mouth and fingers, and I couldn't keep track of what was best, the thick band dipping in and out of my passage or his fingertips working on my clit.

I tugged on his horns, pulling him deeper between my legs. When a growl ripped from him, I paused, lifting my hands away in case I'd hurt him.

Reaching up, he grabbed onto my hands and placed them back on his horns.

"Turns me on," he mumbled, and I somehow understood him. "Going to come if you keep it up."

There was something incredibly arousing in knowing I could turn him on with such a simple touch. So I got into it, sliding my fingertips from the base of his horns to the tips while he pumped his hips, sliding his cock against my lower leg.

He was doing all the tasting, but how could I complain? I wanted him to do this all night. Okay, for breakfast, lunch, and dinner.

How long had we decided we were going to wait before he sunk that big thick cock inside me? Too long.

His tusks scraped across my aroused flesh, and I cried out at the intense sensation. His fingers and tongue alternated, his tongue pumping in when his fingers pulled out, creating a furious rhythm that was going to drive me out of my mind. We were going to go there together.

"Yes," he growled and lifted his head briefly, though the tip of his tongue remained inside me. It could stay there forever. "Keep touching my horns. I'm going to fall apart, my sweetness." He continued to drive his fingers deep inside me. "See how you take them. That's two, but I think you can handle three, don't you?"

They were as thick as every part of this amazing orc, but if he said I could take it, I was going to let him do it.

The stretch made me gasp, and he paused, looking up at me, looking so silly with part of his tongue still inside me.

"Too much?" he mumbled.

"Hell, no."

He grinned. "Did you, my prim and proper librarian, just swear?"

My heart swam from his teasing, melting into a big puddle inside my chest. "If I shout fuck, what will you do?"

"I'm going to give you that too as soon as our waiting period is over, and you're going to take my cock as sweetly as you're now sucking on my *four* fingers."

"Four? Fuck..." I moaned, shoving my hips up to meet each thrust of his hand.

"You're so wet. I love it." Diving back down, he somehow slipped his tongue inside me along with his fingers. I felt stretched to the limit but seeing his erect cock not long ago told me he was even bigger. It was going to feel amazing when he sunk it deep inside me.

When I thought I couldn't take any more, that I was going to shatter into a million fragments of Bailey, he pushed me for more, his fingers and tongue going faster.

"Shoulda sucked on your clit the moment we met," he snarled.

"Before or after I hit you with a stapler?" How could I find the wits to think, let alone speak?

"Both." He moved his hand faster, tipping his gorgeous face up to watch mine. Our eyes locked together. "You're beautiful. Come for me."

And I did, my back arching, and my body spasming like it never had before. My pussy sucked on his fingers, his tongue, and I blasted out a cry of intense satisfaction.

He growled, and I felt his cock jerk against my leg, spurting thick strands of seed onto the grass.

He was right. Orcs did produce a lot of cum.

16

KATAR

We went back inside and after feeding Mozzie and turning out the lights, we snuggled together in her bed.

I'd never felt as satisfied in my life, and I knew it would only get better. When I claimed her fully, she'd truly learn the meaning of wild. My sweet mate would find pleasure over and over soon.

Waking before Bailey, when the sun was just peeking above the horizon, I rose onto my elbow and watched her sleep. Seeing her so completely relaxed was like being reborn again, finding myself in her.

The feeling fired my urge to protect her.

I slipped from the bed and padded out to the kitchen, rubbing my hands together and then pulling things out of her fridge to make breakfast. I'd place a food order later. No way was I going to chow through all she had without replacing it tenfold.

She strolled into the kitchen while I was stirring

scrambled eggs and juggling slices of bread in the toaster. I'd already cooked a bunch of sausage links and toasted half a loaf of bread, but I was a big boy. I ate hearty.

Her yawn stretched out, and she shifted as she leaned against the arched opening to the kitchen, the very short nightie she'd donned moving in a way that made me want to slip it up over her head and toss it aside.

Actually . . . I popped the toast that wasn't finished and shut off the stove burner, then strode over to her, taking her hand and tugging her all the way into the kitchen.

"Looking amazing today, my Bailey." Because she was mine. All I needed to do was claim her and love her for the rest of our days.

I swept the few remaining items off the island.

Bailey frowned as she watched papers go flying. "What—"

Lifting her, I placed her on the smooth surface, an amazing thing since this put her at my level.

I claimed her mouth, teasing my lips across hers, demanding entrance, tasting the minty flavor on her tongue. Moaning, she complied, her hands fluttering on my shoulders before she latched on, digging her nails into my skin.

Yes, like that, my pretty mate.

While my tongues entwined with hers and my cock roared in approval, I slid my fingers up beneath her gown.

Our mouths still fused together, she hitched her hips side to side, dragging up her nightie.

I laid her back on the island and kept that gown going until I could rip it up over her head, find her mouth with my own once again, and stroke both of her breasts.

Her legs were splayed wide, and later I'd make a sacrifice to the fates because, damn, this woman wasn't wearing anything beneath that skimpy nightie.

She ran her hands up and down my arms before stabbing them into my hair, stroking and tugging and driving me straight out of my mind. When I left her mouth, she growled in a needy way that made my poor cock slam against my abs, demanding entrance to the good stuff.

I kissed down her chest and stopped at her right breast to suck her nipple into my mouth. I shifted my face back and forth, rubbing my tusks across it, and I was rewarded when it hardened to a tight bud.

Tugging her to the edge of the island, I spread her legs wide and stepped between them, placed *my hand* between them.

She was incredibly wet. Swollen with a need I was more than willing to satisfy.

"You're amazing," I purred, sucking on her nipple again in a greedy way.

I stabbed two fingers inside her.

She cried out, clutching my horns, rubbing them in a way that made my cock throb and everything inside me tighten.

Because I didn't care about the meal I'd prepared; because I only wanted to eat her, I kissed across her belly and, with a grin, lifted her legs onto my shoulders.

"Hold on, sweetheart. I'm about to feast."

"About? Get doin', sweetheart," she quipped, and I'd never loved her more than I did at this moment.

Loved?

Yeah. I embraced the feelings roaring through me just like I embraced her. This was the norm for orcs and their mates. They were each other's perfect match, so why fight the stampede of feelings when only this person had been picked by the fates for us?

I dove between her legs, dragging my nose through her wetness, drinking in how saturated she was, how amazing she smelled. I'd never get enough, but I was going to eat my fill this morning.

Then I proceeded to lick and suck and nibble on her clit.

She thrashed and moaned, and there wasn't a better sound than my mate finding satisfaction from my touch.

Because I already knew that she liked it, I pumped my fingers inside her, adding a third and the fourth like last night, twisting and turning them to make sure I stroked every bit of her inside walls.

Her clit was a work of art, slightly round yet peaked, and I swore I could feel it throbbing from my touch.

I could feel her body cresting, her inner walls tightening, sucking on my fingers, and I licked harder on her clit, flicking my head back and forth to stroke it with my tusks.

And when she shrieked and clamped down on my horns tightly, I fuckin' almost came in my pants.

Gentling my strokes on her clit, I continued to pump my fingers inside her, riding her orgasm for everything it was worth until she collapsed on the counter.

I gave her one final swipe of my tongue from her opening to her clit and leaned back, sighing while looking up at her.

"I need to do that again very soon, mate, so rest up."

17

BAILEY

Bliss had a name, and it was Katar. My legs shook where they were hooked on his shoulders, and my heart had flung itself apart to let this gorgeous orc saunter inside.

I'd only met him yesterday. How could I be falling in love with him already?

Yet, here I was, eager to tell him he was more than welcome to feast again. Even in my limpness. Even when I couldn't do so much as move. I lay splayed out for him on the counter, and I'd be happy to remain here for the rest of the day.

"Breakfast or me again?" he asked quite politely.

A glance at the clock told me I was going to be late for work already. While today's volunteer, Carole, would open up if I wasn't there, she'd rightly frown when I stumbled through the door. What could I tell her? I was late because the orc I met the day before decided to dine on me instead of the breakfast he'd painstakingly prepared?

"I sense hesitancy on your part," he said, though with an easy grin. "It's all right. A few days. I can wait."

I wasn't sure I could. Maybe he could stop by the library later today, and we could disappear among the stacks. I'd never contemplated having sex inside the library, but there was a first for everything, right?

"It's eight-thirty," I said. "I slept in."

"As you should." He gently removed my legs from his shoulders and helped me sit up. "You'll need the sleep."

Frowning at him, I tilted my head. "Oh? Why in particular?"

"Because I have a few more plans for us that'll show you how wild you can be." My heart floundered, wondering what he'd come up with next. He turned and calmly strode over to the stove. "I assume you need to leave for work soon, sweetheart."

Umm . . . Umm . . . Was I supposed to be able to think after what he'd just done? "Yes, I, uh, do."

"Go shower fast." He paused. "Oh, no, wait."

I slid off the island but leaned against it. "Wait?"

"*Don't* shower."

"Why not? I . . . need to shower each morning. Wash my hair. Wash . . . other parts."

He turned back and strode over to me, pressing me back against the counter. "You can comb your hair. Wash it in the sink, I guess. Get dressed."

"Thanks?" I'd never needed a male's permission to do self-care.

"I want you to leave your pretty little pussy just as it is, dripping from my mouth and the juices your body gave me."

Talk about swoon. It was all I could do not to melt on the floor. "That sounds . . . messy."

"And wild."

Ah, there was that word again.

"I'm going to come see you today," he said. "When's your lunch break?"

I gazed up at him, loving how he looked at me as if he would love to place me back on the island and go for another round. "Thirty minutes at one."

"Be ready for me, then." With that, he turned and sauntered back to the stove. "I'll make you an egg and toast sandwich you can take with you to eat during your drive."

"I usually just stop for egg white bites and a coffee on the way."

"You're going to need something heartier than egg white bites, sweetheart."

My skin tingled from his words, though I wasn't completely sure why.

"Oh?" I asked.

"Oh, yes." He looked back at me over his shoulder. "When I get there, I'm going to lock the door and lay you out on your desk. Then I'm going to have you for lunch."

With my breath coming in jerky pants, I staggered down the hallway and to my room where I fumbled around for something to wear. A skirt. A nice blouse to match.

And no undies.

PANDEMONIUM REIGNED when I got to the library, pulling into my spot at exactly one minute after nine.

Like a good girl, I'd eaten the sandwich he'd prepared for me on my way to work, and man, was it tasty. There was nothing better than an orc eating you out on the island to work up an appetite for . . . Okay, *more*.

But we'd agreed my going wild didn't only apply to my sexuality, and I was eager to find out where he'd take me next. Dancing to the music of the moon and the stars had felt freeing. What else did this orc have to offer?

My coffee—also Katar-prepared—in hand, I strode up the walk with my briefcase in hand, meeting up with Carole out front. My body still hummed, and I swore I smelled from Katar's attentions, but that was the whole point. Every time I sat or moved, I was going to be reminded of what he did to me and what he planned to do to me during lunch.

"The detective is here," Carole said, shooting a look of concern toward the front door. "He's not letting anyone inside."

Oh, yeah. I'd completely forgotten about Detective Carter's visit.

A mom with two children in hand gave me a look of desperation. "They need story hour," she said.

Which Carole would run this morning.

"*Really* need story hour." Her voice lifted to a screech.

"We're holding story hour, no worries," I said with an easy smile.

Funny how a solid orgasm could make a day perfect. I wasn't even stressed that I was already behind.

"Oh, thank God," the mom said, her posture loosening. "It's the only time when I can do my homework." At a lift of my brow, she explained. "I'm taking classes toward a degree at the community college, and during story hour, well, I get a lot done."

"You should bring them in the afternoons for choo-choo book play," I said.

"What's that?"

"We lead them around the library like they're part of a train—complete with cardboard boxes painted to look like boxcars. Then we help them pick out the books they'll read all on their own. We sit them down and help those who are new readers sound out the words. We've got a full staff of volunteers during choo-choo book play. You shouldn't miss it."

"How long does it last?" she asked.

"An hour as well."

"Ah!" She danced in place, her boys looking up at her and giggling. "I'll—we'll—be there."

"Awesome." I turned my smile to the elderly woman waiting patiently beside the door.

"I was about to borrow the next book in the Monster-ville series," Betty Sleed said primly. Eighty years old but still biking to the library every other day, she adored and ripped through every monster romance we stocked on the "steamy" shelf. "I finished My Orc-y Breaky Heart last night at two in the morning, and I'll gnash my dentures if I can't get the next book in the series ASAP."

I hoped it wasn't already checked out, though we had two copies.

I gave her a big smile. "Orcs are amazing, aren't they?"

She wiggled her gray eyebrows. "I'll say."

"Orcs?" Carole asked as I opened the front door and waved for Betty to enter. "Hold on." She slid her arm between Betty and the foyer. "I'm really sorry, but I told you that no one can enter the library yet." Her frantic gaze met mine. "Detective's orders."

"The steamy shelf is near the front, far enough away from the . . . turmoil," I said. "I'm sure the detective won't mind."

Betty huffed at Carole and, with a lift of her nose, pranced inside the library. I hid my smile and followed her, grateful there was still a copy of the next book in the series on the shelf.

"All of you need to wait outside. Please." Detective Carter strode forward, his hands lifted.

"I'm afraid we're already in." I stepped between him and our patrons who poured inside and rushed to various rooms. A library was a thriving business. Surely the detective could see that. If we didn't open, many would mourn—especially the mom with two lively young boys.

"But, but . . ." he said.

I ducked over close to him and lowered my voice. "Is there a problem?"

"Well, it's not huge." His face darkened, and his voice stiffened. "I need to speak with you inside your office."

"I'll handle the desk," Carole said, aiming that way. James Turner, one of our regulars, already stood in front of it with a big pile of books. He was researching ancient Tibet for a paper he was writing for his dissertation, and he must've found more material among our very extensive collection.

Helga Merryweather had been quite particular about

the books she ordered. She'd had a knack for knowing what our patrons might need, even in the future.

It was my job to try to step into her very big shoes.

I followed the detective down the hall to my office and shut the door behind him.

"I do apologize for the mess I didn't create," I said, removing a stack of books from the guest chair and nudging my chin toward it. "Please sit."

He settled on the wooden surface but didn't lean back, watching as I walked around my desk and dropped onto Helga Merryweather's also very big chair.

We went through what I was doing last night when I heard noises in the attic, and how long I was away from my office. I could tell we weren't discovering anything new.

After finishing, he sat for a long moment, staring at me, before nodding slowly.

"I'm afraid you're not going to be happy with the conclusion I've come to," he said.

I nodded politely, wishing he'd get to it so I could do some work. I needed to straighten my office. Do an inventory of the items in the attic and here.

Clean off my desk for my lunchtime visitor.

Detective Carter pulled something from his pocket, and it clinked when he waved it in the air. "I'm afraid, Ms. Everhard, you're under arrest for the theft of the ancient orc tome."

18

KATAR

I arrived at the library not long after Bailey. After cleaning up the kitchen, there was no place I'd rather be. Besides, I had to do some investigating, and that couldn't take place inside Bailey's house until she'd done a full inventory. I did, however, explore outside her house, though I didn't find anything that might tie the break-in to the book's theft.

Striding down the hall, my very good orc hearing picked up the detective's words.

I flung the door open and stepped inside, taking in Bailey gasping and reeling back in her chair and the detective lifting a pair of handcuffs. She stood and scooted around to press her back against a bookcase.

"If Bailey's going to be wearing these, I'm the one who'll be applying them." I gave her a stern look. "And it won't be here inside the library but in the safety of her own . . ." It probably wasn't a good idea to let on that Bailey and I were mates.

"Excuse me." Detective Carter rose to his feet. "You

have no say in this." His scorn-filled gaze landed on her. "Your grandfather would be ashamed of you."

I lifted my brow ridge. "Grandfather?"

"He was the lead detective in town until he retired, and Detective Carter took over," she said, her face scalding red. "He died years ago."

"*I've* done a better job," the detective said with a huff.

"You'll never win the Good Citizen Award. They said they'd never give it to anyone but him."

The detective fumed. "We'll see about that."

Tears shimmered in her eyes. "And my grandfather would *not* be ashamed, because I haven't done anything wrong."

"So they all say." The detective looked up at me. "I came here this morning knowing I'd probably have to arrest Ms. Everhard, and there's nothing you can say that will deter me."

I pulled out my ID and handed it over. "I'm taking over the case. I know the king wouldn't want me to arrest Ms. Everhard."

"You're . . . You're . . ." The detective sputtered. "I saw your name on the information sent by the orc king in the paperwork that came with the tome."

"The king is my uncle," I said with a bite of steel. "We wouldn't want to . . . upset him by arresting his nephew's mate, now would we?"

"Mate?" Detective Carter rose and stumbled away from me—and Bailey, his eyes widening. "You . . . can't be mates. You only recently arrived in town."

Interesting that he knew that, though the information could be public knowledge. "I'm taking over the case.

King's orders and all that. If you need further proof of who I am, you're welcome to speak with the owner of the Seashell Diner. My cousin, Deegar, the former prince of the orc kingdom, or his lovely mate, Cat, would be happy to vouch for me."

The detective blanched. "Oh, I'm . . ."

Bailey slumped in her chair. I hated seeing fear in her eyes, that her breathing was ragged. It was all I could do not to grab the detective by his collar, drag him to the front door, and toss him down the stairs.

While I was given complete discretion to do what was needed in this investigation, I suspected *that* would not go over well with my uncle.

"What evidence do you have to arrest her?" I asked.

"We've reviewed all the film on the cameras." He stiffened, sinking into the role he was more familiar with, that of the lead detective on the case. "No one was seen leaving or entering the library other than the usual patrons during normal hours when, I'll note, the ancient text remained within its glass case. In addition, no one entered after hours last evening, which tells me there was no one inside the attic or her office." His voice rose with indignation. "Outside of library hours, the cameras picked up no one on or near the premises other than her." His finger stabbed toward Bailey. "She must've messed up her office and the attic to throw us off, but we saw through it."

"Why would she need to do that?"

"To distract us. Make us think someone else is involved." He stalked toward her. "Where's the ancient book? We know you've got it, or we hope you do. You didn't sell it already, did you?" He looked my way. "If so, it's in a wealthy person's collection already, and we'll never get it back unless she," he released a snarl, "reveals who she sold it to."

"I didn't steal it," Bailey wailed, looking at me. "You believe me, don't you? I didn't do it. I didn't sell it. I'm a librarian. I take pride in my work and in the legacy Helga Merryweather gently place in my hands."

"I know you didn't steal the book." There was a reasonable explanation, and I was going to find it. "She didn't mess up her office and attic either."

"I did not," she said with a huff, rising to her feet. She wiped the tears from her eyes. "And I certainly didn't break into my own home and rummage through my things."

"You did that to throw us off too." He held up a second pair of cuffs. "You're under arrest."

"I told you I'm covering the case now," I said, taking those cuffs as well. My voice came out so deadly, every orc in the vicinity would freeze if they heard it. "I've built a solid rep for following through on whatever I promise, and if you don't leave now and take your accusations with you, I won't be responsible for how I behave."

"Are you threatening me?" the detective hissed.

Carole ducked her head inside the cracked open doorway. "Is everything okay in here? I heard shouting." Seeing the distress on Bailey's face, she stalked inside and over to my mate, wrapping her arms around her. "What the hell is going on here?" Her gaze stabbed the detective. "I'm not only on the board of the library, but I've made a sizeable donation to the town each year for the past five.

If you so much as threaten one hair on Bailey's head, you and the mayor will be able to hear me shriek and you won't like what the mayor has to say."

I loved that she was defending my mate. "You need to leave," I growled at the detective.

He sputtered. "She needs to be arrested."

When I rushed toward him, he scooted around Bailey's desk and raced for the door. As he hit the hall and started down it, he called out over his shoulder. "You'll see! I'm not letting this go. Bailey Everhard will be locked behind bars before the day is through."

19

BAILEY

I slumped in my chair, the wind completely knocked out of me. My hands and knees shook. I looked up at Carole, who had a fierce, defensive expression on her face. Katar looked ready to go after the detective to rip off his head.

"That's not going to happen," Carole said, her hand landing on my shoulder to give it a squeeze. "You're the last person in the world who'd ever steal the orc manuscript."

"Thank you."

Katar came over and stooped down in front of me, taking my hands and squeezing them. "Who else has access to the library, and is there any other way inside other than the front and back doors?"

"I have a key, as does every member of the board," Carole said. "Any of us could be the perp, but it's not Bailey."

He lifted his brow ridge. "You're suggesting we should be looking at you instead?"

Her face pinkened. "Not really, but I'm pointing out that anyone could have gotten inside and stolen the ancient text."

"They weren't picked up on the cameras," I said.

"We need to examine the footage ourselves and make sure no time is missing." Katar straightened, though he kept a hold of my hands. They were so cold. And my teeth chattered. He stroked my face. "I want to rage around the place, roaring."

That would make me feel marvelous, but it wouldn't solve this big problem.

I was going to jail. They'd lock me up and throw away the key. No one was going to believe I wasn't responsible for the theft. My grandfather, who I didn't even remember, would roll over in his grave.

"Who has access to the hard drive where the data's stored?" Katar asked, peering around the room.

"It's in the hallway closet." I shrugged. "Anyone could gain access, I guess. The storage door's locked, but I keep the keys in my desk drawer. I'm in and out of my office all the time. I try to remember to lock it when I leave, but most of the time, I forget."

I reached forward and slid open the drawer, gasping.

The keys weren't there.

Scooting my chair around Katar, I rummaged inside the drawer. "They were here yesterday. I needed more paper for my printer," I waved to it sitting on a low table near the window, "and this is where I keep it." I looked up at Katar and Carole. "I know I returned the keys."

"Someone was inside the library last night," Katar said, glancing toward the ceiling. "We were in and out, and they could've accessed the hard drive at almost any time. Wiped out any evidence they were here. Is there a backup?"

I frowned. "Maybe. Let's go look."

We left my office. The chatter echoing from the library sounded completely normal, which contrasted sharply with the new turn my life had taken.

"I should go back to the desk." Carole stared into my eyes. "Are you all right? Really? Because I can go put a note there and come back. I'm with you for as long as you need me."

What would I do without my friend? "I'm fine." Not truly, but as long as Katar kept hold of my hand, I would be.

She looked at me a bit longer before sucking in a breath and nodding. "Call out, and I'm bailing on the desk, okay?"

"Thanks." I brushed her hand that had returned to my shoulder. "I appreciate it. But you're only on the schedule for a few more hours."

"I'm here for as long as you need me." She smiled. "Remember, no job?"

Katar frowned, looking between us.

"Carole . . ." Actually, it wasn't my place to say anything.

"I inherited money from my family," Carole said breezily. "I don't need to work. But I can't sit around, you know, doing nothing but spend it. I volunteer here at the library as well as the animal shelter in town."

"She's amazing," I gushed. "And even more, you're a true friend."

"That I am." She bit down on her lip, clearly uncertain about leaving me.

"Go," I said. "Katar and I will do some investigating."

"Okay." Carole left, hurrying toward the front of the library.

We went to the storage closet door, finding it unlocked. "Maybe the detective took the key. I showed it to him months ago when the tome was stolen."

"Maybe." The frown hadn't left Katar's face. "Or maybe whoever was in the attic last night stole the key."

"The detective must've downloaded the camera footage months ago."

I nodded.

"I'll still notify him of this latest bit of evidence."

"He won't care. He's closed the case and named me the culprit."

Katar nudged me against the wall and gently cupped my face. "You didn't do anything wrong. We're going to prove it. And we're going to figure out who stole the book and make them pay for framing you."

"You think that's what this is?"

"All the so-called evidence the detective's counting on points to you, so I'd say yeah."

"Thank you for believing me."

Leaning forward, he kissed the tip of my nose. "Always."

I stiffened my spine, opened the storage closet door, and we stepped inside. I slid the bucket holding a mop and cleaning supplies to the left and waved to the shelf at eye-level on the right holding the computer that stored the images recorded on the many cameras covering the outside of the library. "We should've had cameras pointed at the book."

He nodded thoughtfully, his gaze on the hard drive. "You didn't?"

"Someone on the board said the outside cameras would be enough."

Katar froze and looked back at me. "Who?"

I tilted my head, trying to remember, but I couldn't. "I'm not sure. We can ask Carole if she remembers."

"Do you have a thumb drive?" he asked.

"In my office." I went and grabbed it, thankful to find it still there, and gave it to Katar.

He inserted it into the front of the hard drive and pressed some buttons.

"You appear quite at home with all this." I waved to the whirring device.

"I am" He shot me a grin. "I know what some might think. Orc. Kingdom far beneath the ground. Since the first orcs to emerge from below the ground wore loincloths and were carrying nothing but handcrafted swords, I don't blame anyone for assuming we're a primitive species."

"I wish I'd been there," I said wistfully.

"When we emerged?"

"Were you with them?"

"Yes, why?"

I grinned. "Because there isn't anything I'd like more than to see you wearing a loincloth and bristling with weapons."

20

KATAR

Just like that, my attention left the computer and centered on my mate, who gazed at me with so much heat, it kicked my cock into action.

I groaned.

"Sorry," she said, her smile widening. "I believe," her finger pointed to the bulge forming in the front of my pants, "I've stirred things up."

"You, mate, are going to soon see how stirred up I truly am." Leaving the computer to finish downloading to the thumb drive, I lifted her and pressed her against the wall, making a mop fall onto the floor with a clatter.

As her legs coiled around my waist, I kissed her deeply, gliding my tongue across her lips, demanding entry. She complied with a whimper of surrender. This woman could turn me into a raging inferno in seconds, and I knew she always would. It wasn't just the bond driving us both. It was her. Me. Us.

As I teased her tongue with mine, I gripped her ass with one hand, holding her up, while sliding the other to her breast. I rolled the nipple through her sedate top, and my reward was her jutting her hips against my waist.

Leaving her mouth, I kissed along her jawline to her ear. Human ears were so different from an orc's. Ours jutted up from our head beside our horns, and they came to a point at the top. Some orcs' ears flopped over, but I'd inherited mine from those in the royal family. Points were considered superior, but I didn't care about anything like that.

I just loved it when Bailey grabbed onto them and tugged. When she left them to latch onto my horns.

Heat shot to my cock, and it stiffened even further. How was I going to make it until tonight without claiming her?

I nipped on her rounded earlobe while sliding my hand beneath her top and the stiff garment beneath, shoving it aside to place my palm fully against her breast.

Gasping and arching her back, she yanked on my horns.

I left her perfect ear and made my way back to her mouth, taking it once more.

I stroked her breast and left her lips to yank up her top with my tusks to gain full access to that hard nipple, sucking it inside my mouth and coiling my tongue around it to tug.

"Katar," she cried out, thrusting her hips against me.

Something banged on the hall, and we sprung apart.

Bailey shot me a wild look and smoothed the hair I'd totally mussed. She dragged her skirt back into place and tucked her top back into her skirt. The lovely nipple I'd been working on poked against the fabric.

"You." Speaking sternly, she poked her finger my way. "Behave."

"Do I have to?" I purred by her ear.

Her laugh burst out, though it was jittery. "Hold those thoughts and," she stroked her fingertip down the length of my cock trying to slice its way through the front of my pants, "and keep this big boy nice and toasty. I believe *someone* got to do a lot of tasting, but I have not yet had my fill."

With that, she left the storage closet, striding confidently out into the hall. I was glad she wasn't upset, though I hadn't intended to provide a distraction when I got lost in her mouth.

With a shake of my head, I returned to the computer, finding the thumb drive wasn't big enough to hold all the data. I'd have to get another, which meant a trip to the nearby box store.

Out in the hall, I found Bailey talking with Flynn, the guy who'd stopped by the day before. The one who'd laid a proprietary gaze on my mate and who'd delivered a scowl my way.

That same gaze was now locked on Bailey's breasts.

"Flynn," she said, her voice rising. She snapped her fingers between their bodies. "Flynn!"

"What?" he asked, still focused on her chest.

"My eyes are up here." Pure exasperation came through in her words, and she pointed to her glasses.

"Mine," I growled, stalking over to stand with her, facing Flynn. Would Bailey get upset if I tackled him? If I was dressed in a loincloth and armed with my blades, I would pull them. Brandish them in his face.

Then I would drive him through the front of the library with a warning to never return.

"It's . . . okay, Katar," she said, all breathy. I suspected my prim and proper Bailey didn't enjoy me acting jealous, so I restrained my hands from locking around his throat.

I was an orc. As far as humans were concerned, acting uncivilized came with the territory. But I didn't want to displease my mate.

"What can I do for you, Flynn?" Bailey asked. Did I hear laughter bubbling in her voice?

Like a pup who'd been told he was behaving nicely—now—I sent him a sharp smile that told him I was only tolerating his presence around my mate because she appeared willing to speak with him.

"I heard you were being arrested," he blustered. "I had to come to the library immediately to make sure everything was all right."

Everything? Why not make sure *Bailey* was all right?

"As you can see," she said, "I wasn't arrested."

"Why not? From what I heard; they have plenty of evidence." He stared down his nose at her. What a switch, to go from gaping at her breasts—that were also mine—to acting like he had some say in all this.

"Why don't you leave?" I barked.

Bailey laid a hand on my arm, squeezing it. "Flynn's the chairman of the board, as I mentioned yesterday. It's in his interest to know what's happening with the library."

"I'm grateful you haven't been arrested," he said, his

gaze shooting to her fingers now stroking my bare fore-arm. Did she realize she was doing it?

"So am I."

"I've taken over the case," I said, watching him. This male had a key to the library. Was he somehow involved?

"Why you?" Flynn asked, turning his stiff gaze my way.

"I was assigned by the orc king," I said.

Flynn sucked in a breath. "You know the orc king? I thought you were an innocent bystander who was conveniently here to assist Ms. Everhard."

"I'm investigating the case, hence taking it over from Detective Carter."

"Then you're the reason Ms. Everhard hasn't been arrested?"

"I sure am," I said with an edge of impatience in my voice. This male could leave. I had an investigation to conduct. Bailey to lick.

"Don't you think that's improper?" he asked.

"Me taking the case? I assure you," I said in a deadly tone, "I'm well qualified to handle this investigation."

"I meant since you and Ms. Everhard—"

My snarl broke through his words. I advanced on him, making him back against the wall, his hands fluttering at his throat. "What were you about to accuse *Bailey* of?"

"Nothing," he sputtered. "Absolutely nothing. I'm sure you two are just . . . friends."

"It's all right." Bailey leaned into my side. "You can release him."

That's when I realized I had him by the throat. I'd

lifted him off the ground and his feet were twitching in the air.

I dropped him, and he straightened the neckline of his stiff white shirt.

He scurried toward the front of the building, shooting a dark look my way and delivering a parting shot. "Don't think you'll get away with manhandling me, sir."

21

BAILEY

A shaking wreck for yet another reason, I flopped in my chair inside my office. "You shouldn't have done that."

Katar shut the door and leaned against it. "What in particular?"

"You know. Flynn's an important person here in town. He has a lot of say when it comes to the library." I sighed. "If he gets mad enough, he could have me fired. I'm skating on thin ice already."

"How did he learn you were about to be arrested?"

"That's a question without a good answer. I assume his scanner. Yesterday, he mentioned having one."

"Would the detective announce something like this on a scanner?" I asked.

"Announce that they were arresting me? Probably not." I felt like sobbing. My life appeared to be spiraling down the toilet, and there didn't seem to be anything I could do about it. Katar had held the detective off, but if he found a way to go above Katar, I'd soon find myself fingerprinted and sitting in a jail cell, awaiting a speedy trial.

"It's going to be alright." He tugged me off the chair, sat himself, and lifted me onto his lap, holding me. "I'm here with you, for as long as you need me."

What if I needed him forever?

Now *that* was me going wild. I'd only known him about twenty-four hours, and I was already seeing him as my lifetime. Talk about being out of my mind.

"Stress," I said. "That's why."

"Why are you trembling?" He kissed the top of my head. "We're going to solve this crime and clear your name."

"I don't know what I'd do without you."

"You'd handle this. I've already seen how strong you are, how determined."

"That's me channeling Helga Merryweather. *She* was the strong one. I . . . tend to limp out. Skitter away. I'm a librarian, though prim and proper doesn't necessarily come with the title. But I'm basically a walking librarian cliché."

"You're perfect the way you are. You know that, right? I know you want to go wild, and I appreciate that, but you don't have to do anything but be yourself to impress me."

Now I was getting all warm and mushy, and I *was* going to cry. "You say the sweetest things. Please promise me you're not a rogue."

Tilting his head, he frowned down at me. "Rogue?"

"A rascal or scoundrel. When applied to a male, it means someone who takes advantage of women. Use 'em and lose 'em. I'll call ya sometime. That kind of guy."

His frown didn't smooth. "Would you like me to provide references?"

"If I said yes, who would you give me one?"

"What could be better than a reference from the king of the orcs?"

"I imagine he's an impressive guy."

"Not a rogue," he said with a laugh.

"All that aside, I'm telling you that I trust you not to hurt me."

"You're my mate. I'm merely waiting for you to tell me when it's time to claim you."

"I know claim must mean having sex, but what else comes with an orc mating?"

"Me," he said smugly. "You get all of me."

"That still sounds sexual." And the idea was heating me up nicely. Wrong place. Right guy, however.

"In many ways, it is. But it also means I'll protect you, cherish you, and provide whatever you need for the rest of your life. Following orc traditions, I'll continue to woo you every day of our lives. I'll take care of your home and yard, hoping they'll be our home and yard, and I'll cook for you."

"Do you vacuum?" I was only teasing.

"I do it naked."

Now that was something I had to see. I could picture him dancing around to music through earbuds, sashaying his gorgeous butt and his cock . . . "Would you please vacuum when we get home tonight?"

He flashed his tusks my way. "Only if you'll go wild and use a feather duster while I do it."

22

KATAR

We cooled things down after that. With so much going on, it didn't make sense to keep the heat in high gear until we'd figured some of this out and gotten to know each other better.

That night, we had dinner and sat on the sofa with Mozzie, talking about our lives. I wanted to know everything about her, from her favorite color—orc green—to what she loved doing most in her spare time—reading and taking walks on the beach. We slept together in her bed, and I held her while she cried. I stroked her back when she had nightmares about being locked up in jail.

I wanted to rip the detective's head off, something I was pretty sure would get me in trouble. But he'd hurt her. Made her sad.

Scared her.

And I wasn't going to allow him to do it again.

Each morning, we had breakfast like a couple who'd been together for years.

I liked it. It was calming. Soothing. As perfect as her.

Two days later, after picking up a larger thumb drive, I finished loading all the footage off the library's cameras and strode into Bailey's office.

"Your computer was stolen, but do you have another one in the library?" I asked, holding up the drive. "I want to go through all the footage around the time the book was stolen and when someone was inside the attic."

"There's one at the front desk." She rose. "Speaking of front desk, I really should relieve Vera." She glanced at the big, tall, wooden clock. "I was supposed to take over for her at eleven."

"I'll start scanning the footage and do more investigating outside." So far, I hadn't found any evidence, and I couldn't figure out why. I was missing a clue, and I hoped it revealed itself soon. I doubted the detective would wait much longer before insisting he had his perp, and it was his duty to arrest her.

Thankfully, we hadn't heard from him yet. If he were wise, he'd let me handle this now.

I doubted he was wise.

"I'll let Vera go," Bailey said. "Carole will be here at noon to take over, but there's a gap in the schedule. I usually have my lunch when Carole gets here." Her gaze slid to her desk.

There was nothing I wanted more than to give her the pleasure I'd promised her a few days ago. And I would, tonight. Our plans had changed. Part of protecting my mate included making sure she was no longer under suspicion. I couldn't imagine why anyone would believe this sweet woman was involved in something like this, let alone that she'd sabotage the library to cover it up.

"What time does the library close today?" I asked.

"Four. That's when the last volunteer leaves. I often stay late to catch up on other things, but I'm wiped out. I'll lock up and we can go home then."

"I'm cooking dinner."

"You did last night and the night before that."

"I love taking care of you."

Her lips curled up on one side. "Please tell me you'll cook naked. That apron was mighty cute this morning, but I do believe you'd look even better without it."

"I'm happy to do everything naked, sweetheart," I purred.

"I like that about you. Very much." With that, she turned and sashayed out of the office. I watched her ass because I couldn't help it, then got up and quickly followed her. Hovered over her, actually, but I didn't want to let her out of my sight. So far, her life didn't appear to be threatened but how far would the real criminal go to make sure she paid the price for their crime?

She relieved Vera, who shot me a look I couldn't define. "Would you like me to let Mozzie out for you on my way home?" she asked Bailey.

"Thanks. He'll appreciate it," Bailey said as she sat at the desk in the main part of the library. She turned on the desktop computer and it hummed.

A woman came up to the desk to check out books, and Bailey gave her a smile.

"Hey," the woman said to me. "I think I know you." She looked over her shoulder. "Rexin, come see who's here." Her smiling gaze returned to me. "I'm Adeline. I'm mated to Rexin, and we run the amusement park in town." She juggled the toddler orcling on her hip. "This little one is Carrie." She kissed the small orcling's cheek while an orc strode from the other room and up to us.

He put his arms around Adeline and leaned over to kiss her neck before looking up at me. "Rexin Tavalog. You're Katar, right?"

"I am."

"Nice to see you again. I believe we met a few years ago at a party."

"I remember." I leaned over to pat his shoulder. "Nice seeing you again."

"You too."

Carrie started to fuss.

"We'd better go," Adeline told Rexin. She shot me a frazzled look. "Nice seeing you!"

They left at the same time as Vera.

I walked over to the window and watched Vera get into a slick blue sports car and drive away. Rexin loaded Carrie into an orcling seat in a large truck, then boosted Adeline into the front seat, rounding his truck to get in on the driver's side.

Movement across the road drew my eye.

Someone stood under a tree across the street, looking this way. Squinting, I tried to see who it was, though I didn't know many people in town. With the sun slanting this way, all I could catch was that the person was tall. Wearing pants. Maybe a male?

Walking back to the desk, I leaned down to speak in Bailey's ear, wishing I could suck on it. Would the elderly male checking out books notice? Probably. Grumbling, I restrained myself. "I'm going to step outside for moment," I whispered.

She nodded, busy with the male.

Because I never let anyone know I was coming, I ducked out the back door and moved carefully to the end of the back wall, peering around, my gaze trained to where I'd seen the person.

There was no one there.

An orc female pushed a stroller along the sidewalk, an orcling inside kicking its feet and squealing. A young human male rode a board with wheels in the opposite direction on the street, and two cars passed the library.

I didn't see anyone who might be the watcher. Assuming there was a watcher. Maybe it was someone who'd stopped and thought of going to the library and changed their mind.

Or they were entering right now . . .

Adrenaline roaring through me, I bolted inside, stomping down the hall to the entryway.

One woman stood there while a second woman was shutting the front door. They both looked my way, one reeling back as if I'd attack her.

"We . . . We . . ." the first said. "Run, Jenny. Run!"

The second wrenched open the front door and they raced out, slamming the door closed behind them.

"Greeting the patrons?" Bailey stood in the opening to the main room, her eyes sparkling with humor.

"They, um, changed their minds," I said sheepishly.

"Maybe they'll change their minds again and come back." Her smile didn't fade as she turned to return to the desk.

I slunk into the room behind her, striding to the front window to look out again.

The person was back, standing beneath the tree.

Male. I knew this in my bones.

I walked slowly to the back door and did the same thing, creeping to the side of the building to peer around it.

Again, there was no one there.

BAILEY

K atar dragged up a chair, placing it beside mine, and loaded the newly loaded drive into the computer. While he scrolled through the footage, I helped patrons. The volunteer, Sam, who was supposed to help for the afternoon, didn't show. I'd call him tomorrow and make sure he was okay.

Eventually, the patrons left, and we were alone. Seeing it was nearly four, I made sure everyone had left, locked all the doors, and checked the windows, before dropping into my seat next to Katar.

"Find anything?"

"Whoever installed your security system knew what they were doing. There isn't a section outside the library that's not covered." He shook his head. "There's no missing footage, not six months ago when the book was stolen nor when someone was inside the attic. Just as interesting, no one approached the library from any direction when the book was stolen or on the night when you heard someone in the attic."

"So how did the person get inside after hours?"

"Could they have been there all day, waiting for everything to quiet down so they could do a more thorough search?"

"I always make sure everyone's gone before I lock up. There aren't any hiding places. I even check the basement and closets." I frowned. "I'm still trying to figure out why, if we're dealing with the same person, they waited six months before going through my office and the attic. What were they looking for?"

"A very good question." He rose, stretching his arms overhead.

I salivated over his rippling abs revealed by his lifted shirt, my gaze widening. When I licked my lips, because . . . whoa, he groaned and something big stirred in his pants.

"Cock? Meet your match," he growled.

Everything this guy said was hot. I swallowed—hard.

"I'm desperate to discover what else you could do with your plump lips," he said softly. Deadly. My insides burst into flames. "Your tongue. What else you might be willing to swallow."

"I think . . . anything."

"You're perfect."

Never, but I loved that he saw me that way.

"We're alone now, right, Bailey?" he rasped, looking around with a suddenly hooded gaze. "I've missed you over the past few days."

"I . . ." I'd been so frightened after the detective tried to arrest me that I couldn't think of anything else.

Now all I could think about was Katar.

"Perhaps it's time I went wild again," I whispered.

"There's my sweetheart."

My eyes swept up his body in a caress, landing on his mouth.

"Fuck," he groaned. "There's no way I'll ever to be able to walk away from you. You know that, right? No way I'll ever be able to go even one day without being with you completely."

"You say all the best things."

"And I one hundred percent mean them." He took my hand and helped me out of my chair.

Really. I could do that for myself. But it made my knees tremble to think that he wanted to do it for me.

"Where do you want me to suck on your clit, sweetheart?" he asked as if he discussed the temperature outside. "I think I've forgotten what you taste like, and I need a reminder."

"Here?" I looked around wildly. "But . . . we're inside the library."

"Once you lock up, you cease being the librarian, correct?"

I frowned, thinking. Trying to think, that is. "Kinda. Sorta. I mean, I'm still on the premises, but one could say that I can shed my role as head librarian when there are no patrons to assist."

"Is me sucking on your clit inside the library wild enough for you or do you want more?"

I had a feeling I'd always want more.

He must be able to read my thoughts because his eyes literally *smoldered*.

"I guess . . . one might consider you sucking on my clit

against the stacks as wild enough for this moment," I said meekly. How was I finding the will to stand? I was about to turn this into a romance movie cliché and sweep everything off my desk, lay down on my back, and let him suck on whatever he pleased.

With a sultry smile, he led me across the room and down a long row of stacks. "What subject?"

"I'm . . . sorry?" My voice fluttered.

"What subject is most appealing to you?"

"I've always been partial to ancient Egyptian archaeology."

"The Mummy. I saw those movies. That woman is hot."

Jealousy swarmed through me with the sting of a thousand bees, though I had no reason to feel that way. I found her hot too. I sucked in a stiff breath. "Do you believe *she's* as hot as *me*?" I asked way too primly.

"No one," he snarled. "Absolutely *no one* is hotter than you, Bailey."

Ah, well, I guessed I could live with him finding that woman hot as long as I was hotter.

Finding the section I was referring to; he assessed the long row of shelves holding books. "Yeah, this isn't going to work. I could grab a book and suck on your clit while you're lying on it, but . . . Hmm."

"What are you doing?" I asked, a bit stunned. Me, lie on a book while he dove between my legs?

Why had my entire body turned to rubber? I'd had nothing alcoholic to drink.

I was high on Katar.

Orcs really did do it better. Well, the sucking part. I was still awaiting the fucking part.

"There's something about front windows that holds some appeal," he said slyly.

Sensing where he was going with this, I gasped. "Please tell me you're not into voyeurism."

"We could do it in the park. Ever had sex while bent over a bench when anyone could walk past on the path?"

"No!"

"Sad, Bailey. Sad." He led me back through the stacks, speaking over his shoulder. "Would you *want* to?"

Shit, shit, yesssss.

"No," I said firmly. "I'm not that wild."

"Yet, sweetheart. Yet." His eyes smoldered, and I could tell he was thoroughly enjoying teasing me.

And that I was falling in love.

24

KATAR

Reaching the front of the main room, I studied the wall between the windows. This would do.

I turned and leaned against it, trying not to jar the painting of an old male staring sternly at whoever came near.

"That's Mr. Merryweather," Bailey said, pointing. "Helga's father. Quite a stern individual according to Helga."

I studied his face. "He has a long nose."

"I suppose one might call it long."

"He's scowling."

Her lips curled up. "Because he knows you're about to lick my clit right below him."

"Oh, I definitely am." Taking her hand, I switched our positions, pressing her against the wall and claiming her ripe mouth. I devoured her, sucking on her tongue and doing all I could to draw in her moans. "It's been ages since we were together. I'm a starving orc, and I can't wait to consume you."

When I lifted her, pressing her against the flowery paper covering the wall beneath Mr. Merryweather, she clutched my shoulders, but not for long. Her hands roamed to my shirt, yanking it up to place her palms on my abs.

Breaking away from her mouth—a terrible thing right there—I stared down at her.

She gazed at me with so much heat, it burned through me. It centered in my cock, but what else was new?

"I'm going to suck on you," I growled.

"And I'm going to suck on you," she said with an equally ferocious growl.

My grin rose. "My mate."

"Your mate," she agreed.

"Not too soon?"

Her head tilted. "It's been a couple of days since we met, hasn't it? I believe we've backed off long enough."

"Perfect mate." I dove back to her mouth.

She moaned and writhed against the wall as I kissed her, and if we could just stay here forever, I'd be the happiest of orcs.

Placing her on the floor, I deftly slipped off her panties and lifted her skirt. Then, with another tusky grin, I dropped to my knees, lifted her legs onto my shoulders, and dove into her saturated goodness.

25

BAILEY

I was being eaten alive, and he could keep on doing this forever. Who ever said cunnilingus wasn't satisfying hadn't been with Katar. This orc had a magical tongue. He'd woven his way into my soul, and there wasn't anything I could do about it.

Nothing I *wanted* to do about it except hold on to his horns and let it happen.

His tongue dove inside me while his fingers were devoting their lives and charms to my clit.

I cried out, eternally grateful we were alone inside the library. As for the windows on either side of me, let alone Mr. Merryweather gazing sternly down at us, who the hell cared? I was lost in Katar-land, and as far as I was concerned, I never wanted to return to the real world. That place was filled with a tragic upbringing, finding a home with Helga, then losing that as well.

With Katar, I was starting anew.

He drove his wonderful tongue deep inside me,

swirling it around and flicking it, teasing across my inner walls. Freakin' fucking me with it.

I shrieked again, and he tipped his head back to watch me. Utter satisfaction shone in his eyes, and I wasn't doing more than massaging his shoulders. Oh, wait, his horns . . .

I grabbed onto them, then realized the gesture lacked finesse. Taking better care, I teased my fingertips up and down them while he continued driving me to the brink with his mouth.

His groan slipped out when I hit what must be a sensitive part on his horns, a slight dimple I discovered on each side. I focused my attention there, stroking through them like he did with his tongue through my wetness.

My mind had lost all track of anything but me doing finger sex on his horns, him doing tongue sex on me, and how amazing my life was now that he was in it.

I bucked against his mouth and thanked the powers that be for placing this orc in my orbit.

He lifted his head. "Come for me, Bailey. Now." Diving back between my legs, he added a few fingers to his tongue, pumping into me in a way that was going to make me explode in seconds.

"You . . . come for me," I shouted. "This is a two-way street, mate."

He chuckled against my saturated flesh. "All in due time."

"I want you," I cried out. "All of you. It's past time you did some orc claiming, mate."

He stilled and looked up at me, tugging his tongue out, making my clit throb with need. "Are you sure?"

"Completely."

"Mate," he growled, stabbing his tongue inside me again before pulling it back out. "Do you want me here or . . . Or do you want to leave it for tonight's latest adventure into your wild side?"

He expected me to think? Jeez.

"I want both."

His incredible mouth stilled. His fingers stilled, and I whimpered. "Both?"

I nodded.

"Tell me with your big girl words, sweetheart," he purred.

"Fuck me right now, damn you."

"Now there's the prim librarian I've fallen in love with."

My heart flung itself against my ribcage, trying to reach him.

"You're sure here's the right place?"

"Everywhere," I breathed. "Now. I don't want to wait any longer."

"But here, as in the library, between the windows, with Mr. Merryweather watching?"

I'd lost all my inhibitions, and the idea thrilled me. "Can you think of a better place?"

His low laugh rang out. "Alright, then. Why don't we start by putting on a show for Mr. Merryweather. We can go truly wild. After that, I've got some stimulating ideas in store for you, mate."

I didn't doubt it. He possessed a sensuality I envied,

but he'd taken my hand, and he was leading me on a journey I never hoped to come back from.

I was completely Team Katar.

With my legs back on the floor, he shucked his shirt, exposing all those miles of rippling, green-skinned muscles. I stroked his arms and his pecs, wanting to feel every bit of his skin.

Trailing my fingertips down his abs, I stopped at his pants and unfastened the top. He watched me with hooded eyes as I tugged down the zipper and parted the fabric, releasing his cock. It sprang free, thick and long.

Bumps shivered across the darker green surface, and when I teased the tip of my finger across one, it vibrated.

I'd died and gone to heaven, and it was centered in his cock.

"I knot," he growled.

I darted a look up at his face creased with desire. "Knot?"

"After." He touched the tip. "After I come, this part swells, locking me inside you. It's supposed to keep my seed inside to give us an orcling."

Strangely enough, I could picture myself holding a child created from both him and me, a perfect little person we'd share and adore. I wanted that image to be real.

"Condoms?" I asked.

"None fit."

"And what do you do in the orc kingdom?"

"It's rare for us to have any orclings, so no one worries about it."

"I'm on the pill."

When he frowned, I explained.

"So you can't get me pregnant despite your knot," I said.

"I think you're discounting the virility of my seed."

"And I think you're discounting the virility of my birth control."

"Very well." His chest puffed. "Challenge accepted."

My laugh snorted out, silenced quickly by a flash of pure need.

"Your cock seems pretty big already," I said. "How much swelling are we talking about?" I tried to wrap my hand around it, but it was too wide.

"My knot will fill you completely."

He was going to fill me completely just by pushing all this inside me—and I couldn't wait.

Frowning, I leaned over to check out something I saw just above his gorgeous cock. "And what's this?" I was on a voyage of discovery with his body, and man, was he beautiful.

"My spur."

"Oh, hell. You come with your own, built-in sex toy?"

He chuckled. "Sweetheart, I come with two sex toys, and I'm going to give them both to you at the same time." He tapped the spur. "This is going to drive your clit wild."

"That's your tongue's role."

"While I'm pumping inside you from either the front or the rear, my spur will stretch. The tip will latch onto your pretty little clit and suck."

"I'm never going to want anyone else," I said in awe.

"Only me, Bailey." Jealousy burned like a flame in his

dark eyes. "No one else is ever going to place his cock inside your slick wetness but *me*."

I curled my finger to bring his face lower, and when he did, I slid my fingers along his horns, paying particular attention to the erogenous area I'd discovered.

His eyes closed, and a groan ripped through his chest.

"You know what this means?" I asked in a sultry voice.

He snarled and shook his head no.

"That *you* belong to *me*."

In a flash, his hands were all over me, pulling my blouse off, sliding my skirt down over my hips.

Latching onto my hands, he held them above my head against the wall. They banged into Mr. Merryweather's nose, but he could deal.

"Bailey," Katar growled, kissing me, his tusks pressing against my cheeks and my glasses squishing my nose, though I didn't care about either. "I'm going to take you hard and fast. You're never going to want anyone but me."

I'd never been turned on by an alpha, but his words worked, driving heat through me like a red-hot poker, centering in my core that already throbbed for his big cock.

As he kissed along my neck and sucked one of my nipples into his mouth, I arched my back, offering myself to him.

His breathing was ragged, and his gaze scorched my flesh. There was something incredibly powerful about knowing I could turn this male on like no other. And that he could unlock the wildness inside me and set it free.

"I want you so completely enthralled by me that you can't see where you stop and I begin," he growled against my breast. "Can you give that to me? Can you let go and be mine completely?"

My guttural moan ripped out, and I nodded.

"Big girl words, Bailey," he chided, one corner of his mouth curling up. "Tell me what you need."

"You. Take me. Claim me. Show me what I've been missing." I was so far gone already, he'd only have to slide his thumb across my clit, and I'd explode.

His mouth collided with mine, his kiss as wild as the Bailey hiding inside me. Lust coursed through me, but it was so much more than that. This was the start of a fusing of two souls, the beginning of us.

With his palms on my thighs, he lifted me and thrust me against the wall, creating a bang that vibrated through my bones and shifted the portrait above me. Katar stepped between my legs as I curled them around his torso.

He lifted his head. "First, mate, you're going to fall apart for me. Would you do that for me, let me completely possess you?"

"Yes," I breathed.

26

KATAR

My desire was a ferocious beast inside me, but I had to rein it in. The need to possess her completely might drive me over the edge, and the last thing I wanted to do was hurt her. I was big, and she was incredibly small.

And undeniably wet as I slid the tip of my cock through her swollen folds.

I needed to make her wetter. Only then would I drive my cock inside her.

The caress of her fingers on my horns was going to drive me completely out of my mind. My will was a thin thread, precariously close to snapping.

She bucked against me as I sucked on her nipple, and there was no one more amazing than this woman giving into her need.

There was only this moment with Bailey.

I growled against her skin as my cock caught fire, demanding I plunge inside her and claim her just like the orcs of old.

Her hunger met mine in a mad rush, her nails dragging up and down across my chest, igniting a feral need inside me. No one but her would ever be able to make me feel like this again.

As I continued to slide my cock through her slickness, the rug slid out from behind me. I crashed forward, into her, and she only moaned, tightening her grip on my horns.

I slid my hand between us, urging my throbbing cock to the side, and plunged two fingers inside her.

She gasped and her keening cry rang out.

I lifted my head, locking our gazes together, finding the same overwhelming need in her gaze that matched my own. "You're mine, Bailey, as much as I'm yours."

"Yes," she gasped, wiggling and thrusting her pelvis forward to meet each plunge of my fingers.

Skimming my thumb across her clit, I watched her face. She melted into me, pushing her back against the wall to curl her hips up to meet my fingers. My groan roared up my throat. She was so incredibly wet, so incredibly responsive, I was going to come before I sunk my cock within her.

"More," she snarled.

I added a third finger, spreading them to stretch her, twisting them around to touch every bit of her inner walls. She dripped for me, but was it enough?

"You're amazing," I growled against her neck. "You're going to take my cock so well."

"Stop teasing me about it and fucking give it to me!"

My laugh snorted out. Where had my prim and

proper librarian gone? She'd been replaced by a wildcat, and I loved it.

Loved her.

I'd fallen so fast and so deep. There was no turning back. No turning away from Bailey.

I moved my fingers faster, driving them up into her slick core while stroking her thumb with my clit. My cock was on fire and if she kept releasing those moans, I was going to shatter before I'd sunk within her.

When she began to shudder around my fingers, I lifted my head, locking my gaze on hers. I wanted to feel it. See it. And then drink from her pleasure.

"You're amazing, mate," I said again, whispering the words. "Come from my fingers, love, and then I'm going to make you come again from my cock."

She bucked against me, unrestrained and free with need consuming every part of her body.

"Do it," I growled. "Let go. Give it to me."

Her back bowed as she surrendered, and she cried out my name.

27

BAILEY

I was a limp wreck, but we'd just gotten started. His cock was still a thick rod thrusting against his abs and, greedy me, I wanted to feel all of it.

"Mine," I snarled with the wildness he'd unlocked inside me. I grabbed his cock and squeezed. "You're holding out on me, Katar." I was a wire pulled tight, and if he didn't give me everything, I was going to snap.

He unhooked my legs from around his body, and I whimpered when he lowered me to the floor.

"It's not over," I cried as he stepped back.

But he took my hand and squeezed it, and the devilish smile on his face made everything inside me quiver.

"Not over by a long shot." He tugged me behind him, across the big open room of the library and into the foyer. Sometime between Vera leaving, him looking over the camera footage, and him finger fucking me between the windows, it had gotten dark.

He opened the door, and cool night air swept in.

I sobered in an instant. "What—"

"Time to go really wild, Bailey." He took me out the front door and to the right.

"We're outside," I squeaked. "Naked!"

"And you look amazing." He lifted his hand and licked the fingers that had just been driving deep inside me. Coiling his tongue around each of them, he sucked to make sure he got every bit of my wetness. "Amazing."

"Cameras!"

His eyes widened before they smoldered. "I'll erase anything good on the tape."

Alright then.

"I . . . I . . ." Just like that, he could make me fall apart, make me forget we were outside, that anyone could walk by and see us.

"There's a big bush." He waved to it, and yes, it did somewhat block us from the path and the sidewalk.

My car was the only one in the lot, and while the streetlights were lit, the closest pole was on the opposite side of the road. Thankfully, no one was walking by.

He dropped down onto the stone bench on the open deck in front of one of the windows, and patted his lap, his lips curling up around his tusks. "Sit. Ride me, mate. Show me how crazy you can be."

"But someone could see us," I sputtered. Right now, only my eyes were wild, darting from him to the lot to the road.

He shrugged and wrapped his fingers around his cock. "They'll look away."

"I might cry out."

He flashed me a tusky smile. "Oh, you'll definitely cry

out. But I plan to capture your heady sighs and screams with my mouth."

When he put it like that . . .

I pursed my lips. "Promise?"

"Get your pretty ass over here and spread your thighs for me. Show me that wild woman inside who's been begging to get out."

My breath caught. His dirty talk was going to drive me to my knees.

"There's no moon or stars tonight," he added, glancing up. "It's dark enough we shouldn't be seen."

"Shouldn't isn't won't."

"I dare you." He milked his luscious cock with his big hand. "Come suck on this with your pretty little cunt, sweetheart."

"Fuck," I breathed. "If any other male used cunt in relation to my body, I'd smack him."

"Say more dirty things to me, sweetheart."

"I've sworn more in the past few days than the rest of my life combined."

"I like hearing you say fuck. Now trot your sweet little body over here, climb on top of me, and let me show you what you've been missing."

Someone might see. Someone might hear.

And right now, I didn't give a damn.

I was so aroused I was going to explode just standing here watching him touch himself.

No, I was greedy enough, *I* wanted to be the one doing it for him.

Straightening my back, I sauntered over to him, swaying my hips. His smile grew with each of my steps.

"Now there's my amazing mate," he purred, patting his thigh. "She's going to come for me again. I know it."

With that cock and spur? It was guaranteed.

I climbed up onto his lap and straddled his thighs, not quite sure how this would work. The only other time I tried this position, I bounced around while the guy groaned and came, then he urged me off and went to sleep while I lay beside him, fuming, with my body just starting to warm up.

"You're overthinking this." He tipped my chin up so our eyes could meet. "Just feel."

When he slid his hand between us and started rubbing my clit, I caught fire once more. The world around us compressed until it was just him and me.

"Claim me, sweetheart. Ride me hard and get your reward."

"I'm not even sure we'll fit." Gasping, I leaned back, thrusting my hips forward, spreading my thighs further while he dipped a finger inside me. I clutched his sides and rocked against his thumb. "Yes, like that."

His lips curled up before smoothing. "Rise. Settle down on top of me when you're ready. I promise, I'll make sure it sinks all the way inside you."

He was so stiff, and the nubs hummed a low tune that called to me like no other.

I lifted my body and spread myself further, placing the head of his cock at my saturated entrance.

"Yes, like that," he growled. "Tell me when you're ready."

I flashed a look up at his face, pausing to take in how tight it was with need. He'd given me so much pleasure already while ignoring his own needs. He might act all alpha, but inside he was mush—for me.

The thought thrilled me like no other.

I jerked my head in a nod. "I'm ready."

"Then let go."

Releasing my hold on my thighs, I dropped down while he pushed on my hips.

Only a fraction of his beautiful cock sunk inside me.

Whimpering with need, I lifted and let myself fall again, but even now, only part of his cock filled me.

"You promised me," I snarled, my face pinched, my body quivering and shaking with arousal.

His low laugh rang out. "Never fear, sweetheart, I fulfill all my promises."

The next time I rose and let myself go, he jerked his hips up to meet me, driving his glorious cock all the way inside me.

I paused, panting against his warm chest, savoring how wonderful the stretch felt. I was splayed wide for him like a feast.

Then his spur found my clit and started vibrating.

With a gasp, I looked up, my gaze meeting his filled with humor. "Like it?"

"Fuck," I groaned.

He curled forward to kiss me again, lifting his head only enough to speak, his lips teasing mine with his words. "Cry 'fuck' when you come, mate. I need it."

My inhalation shuddered through my lungs, and I nodded.

I was so going to shout fuck.

I started moving, though honestly, he did most of the

work, lifting me with his big fingers wrapped around my waist, then driving me down when I dropped, his cock thrusting up to meet me.

While I whimpered and moaned against his chest, his spur slicked across my clit. I was a dripping wreck, and only this male was going to complete me.

Prissy Bailey? Meet your match in an orc named Katar.

We went faster, him slamming up into me while I clung to his arms and drove myself down. Our bodies were a sweaty blur, and when I started to shudder in his arms, he helped me go faster.

"I have to . . ." I was so far gone; I couldn't complete the thought. I searched for his gaze, finding him watching me, his eyes darkened with need.

"Take it. Bloom with it, Bailey. I'm yours. You're mine. And nothing and no one is going to tear us apart."

The tip of his spur vibrated harder, and pleasure sucked me down in its heady embrace. I came in rolling waves, crashing against the shore over and over while I rode him.

I surrendered everything I was inside to this male alone, handing him my heart and my soul along with my body.

And like he'd promised, he curled forward and captured my mouth, captured my sighs and my cries of pleasure. Captured me bellowing fuck.

When I slumped in his arms, he lifted his head. He growled and slid his fingers down to the bottoms of my thighs, spreading them even farther. Then he pumped his cock up into me in a wild rush, driving so deep, I rocketed up into the sky once more.

I bucked against him, kissing his chest until he bellowed and came deep within me.

My breath flew out all at once, and I gazed up at him. We stared at each other, and his hands rose to gently cup my face.

"Mate of mine?"

"Yes?"

"You've wrecked me, and I can't wait for you to do it again."

I'd never felt as decadent and satisfied in my life.

Our bodies still knotted together, he stood and carried me back inside, kicking the door shut with his heel and twisting the lock. He padded down the hall to my office and settled in my chair like he owned it.

Why not? He'd just owned *me*.

28

KATAR

As much as I wanted to claim my mate in every available location within the library, we had to eat. Sleep. *Then* we could get back to the claiming.

After my knot released, we dressed and left, me scrunching into her tiny car. I needed to buy a truck.

Bailey pulled the vehicle up to an intersection and waited for the light to change color. Such a strange concept to me. Why red for stop and green for go? If anything, red should give someone a sense of urgency and push them to make the vehicle go faster.

She shot me a smile that made my cock perk up and pay attention. "Everything okay?"

Other than the cramp in my right thigh and the crook in my neck, yes.

"I'm fine," I said as she started moving the vehicle forward again. "I was thinking."

"About what?"

Thankfully, her smile held. She didn't doubt us, and I didn't either, but . . .

"Where will we live?" I asked.

"Ah, now that's an interesting question." She lifted the lever beside the wheel and a clicking sound rang out along with yet a different light flashing before her eyes on the car's viewscreen. So many lights. "My job is here. I live here in the house Helga's father built and she bequeathed to me, but I understand what you're saying."

That was good because I wasn't sure what I was saying.

"Would you ever consider moving?" I asked.

"To the orc kingdom?" Her brow tightened. "Maybe. You have books there, so you must have libraries and librarians to curate them."

"We do."

"I'm not opposed to going there with you and seeing what it's like. Would I be welcome there? Orcs seem to be fitting into human society seamlessly."

Now, they were. Things were a little tight in the beginning. We looked completely different from them. We had tusks. Some of us stomped around, growling a lot.

And we were big, towering over even most of the males who played a sport called basketball.

"Would you consider living here if things didn't work out for us there?" she asked, driving the vehicle onto the road that led to hers. Lights came up close behind us, remaining there, and she squinted, shooting a wry look over her shoulder. "Maybe back off there, buddy, and I'll be able to see." She shook her fist in the air. "We're having a conversation!"

My growl rumbled in my chest. Even someone irritating my mate was enough to make my spine stiffen. The rest of me couldn't do so at the moment since I was curled into a ball on her passenger seat.

"I'm not sure," I said, frowning into the blaze of lights behind us.

"Are you saying that if we don't live in the orc kingdom, our mating is over?" she carefully asked.

"Never that," I vowed. "We'll talk and figure this out."

"Alright. I'm open to talking about it."

She turned onto her road.

The engine of the vehicle behind roared, and it raced closer, slamming into the back of Bailey's car. She yelped. I was thrown against the front of the car, ramming my knee into the glass. Fortunately, the glass held. My knees screamed.

"Let me out," I snarled, yanking on the handle that should release the door.

"Sorry. Child locks," she said, slowing the car.

The other vehicle hit us again, and Bailey yanked the wheel, turning the car onto a lawn on our right with the other vehicle right behind us.

"Watch out," she cried, her wide-eyed gaze focused forward.

A tree loomed ahead, and we smacked into it, coming to a shuddering halt.

While Bailey panted and clutched the wheel, I smashed my fist through the window and brushed aside the tiny specks of glass. I crawled through the opening, landing hard on the ground as a male rushed out of the nearby house exclaiming about his tree. Leaping to my feet, I ran toward the back of Bailey's car.

The truck that had hit us—blue—squealed its tires

and flew past us, down the road. It turned a corner and disappeared from view.

"Did you get the plate?" Bailey asked, running over to clutch my arm.

"Plate?"

"The number on the back of the vehicle."

I shook my head.

"Then did you see who the driver was?"

"Tall. Shadowy. It was hard to tell in the lights."

"Male or female?"

"I don't know," I growled, tugging her into my arms. "I'm sorry. I didn't get a good enough look at them."

"It's okay. We're okay." She looked up at me. "You're okay, aren't you?"

I nodded and held her tighter.

All of this was connected—somehow—and I was going to rip this world apart to find out who was after Bailey.

29

BAILEY

Detective Carter arrived in his cop car, bringing it to a screeching halt at the curb and getting out, hurrying over to join us.

"Trying to create more suspicion about someone else to throw us off?" he asked me snidely after I told him what happened.

Katar growled.

Detective Carter took one look at his face and stepped backward.

"Tell Bailey that you didn't mean what you just said," Katar snarled. "Now!"

"Look," the detective said, his hand spreading wide, "we only have your word for it that someone hit the back of your vehicle."

I plucked at the front of his shirt, fisting it, actually, and dragged him over to my car, pointing to the large dents in the back. "This was not here this morning."

"So you say."

I growled this time.

He again took a few steps backward.

"I'm not making this up," I shouted.

"Be reasonable." He huffed. "It's your word against mine, and we know how that'll come out."

"Why are you determined to place all of this on Bailey?" Katar asked in a deadly voice from behind me. "You're not doing your job, which is why I took over."

Detective Carter stiffened and yanked on his uniform jacket. "I've already investigated. The evidence shows no one at the library other than her," his finger stabbed my way, "not only on the night the book was stolen but when she insists someone rummaged through the attic and her office. As for her home, she wouldn't be the first to do something like that to distract a sharp detective on a hot case."

"I was with Bailey while her house was being ransacked," Katar said.

"You're involved with her. Of course you'd say that."

I rolled my eyes. "Are you going to go after the blue truck or not?"

"Whoa. Did you see that?" the owner of the house with the tree said, joining us. He smoothed his hand across the top of his bald head and tweaked the dangling bits of hair on the sides of his moustache. "I saw a big blue truck not only hit this woman's car but drive off afterward."

"You were inside your house," the detective said. "You couldn't have seen all that."

"My dog had to go out. I was standing at the front door, unlocking it, when it all happened. Saw it through the glass myself."

"Ah." The detective frowned. "I'm sure there's a reasonable explanation. Road rage, perhaps? You were driving erratically, or you gave the blue truck's driver the finger. He gave chase, perhaps to make a citizen's arrest."

"You really are a piece of work," I said with disgust. "You should be fired."

"And you should be under arrest!"

The owner of the house backed up, his hands lifting. "Gotta go let my dog out the back door. You folks can settle this without me. Fill out the report and make sure I get a copy for insurance reasons. And just remember, Detective, I saw the truck hit her, driving her car into my tree. Which will probably need to be cut down. Poor thing's got a huge gash in it. Trees have feelings, you know."

We watched as he hurried back inside the house.

Thunder boomed overhead, making me jump, and like a switch had been hit, it started to pour.

"I'll call a wrecker for your car," Detective Carter yelled. "Then come to your house to fill out the report!"

Katar took my hand, and after I'd grabbed my purse and keys from my vehicle, we ran down the street and up onto my covered front porch. We dripped as I fumbled with my keys to find the one for the front door.

The detective's car parked at the curb behind us, and he got out, hurrying up the walk as I slipped the key into the lock. I opened the door and waved for him and Katar to enter ahead of me.

I shut the door and wiped my feet on the mat, though it hardly mattered when I was so saturated, my clothing was flooding the floor.

Detective Carter removed his shoes and took two steps into my living room before coming to a stop. "Well, well, well. What do we have here?"

I peered around him to find the orc manuscript—the one stolen six months ago from the library—sitting on my coffee table in plain view.

30

KATAR

"Ms. Everhard," the detective snarled. "You are definitely under arrest."

"I'm not allowing that to happen," I said, stalking past him and stopping beside the book, peering down at it.

"But . . ." Bailey's hands fluttered at her throat. "I didn't steal it. It wasn't here this morning. Right, Katar? You were here last night—"

"He was?" The detective grumbled and shook his head in disgust. "Fraternizing with the suspects, are you, Mr. Dolkin? I wonder what the king of the orcs would think of that, king's *nephew*."

"I wonder what the king would think about you arresting a woman who isn't guilty of stealing the book," I said.

"It's right there in plain view." When the detective pulled handcuffs from his back pocket and held them up, I snatched them out of his hands.

"I told you no one's cuffing Bailey except me."

"She needs to be arrested," he fumed. "The book is

right here, in her possession. She stole it. We've found it and the case is wrapping up just like that." Detective Carter lifted the book. "I've seen numerous photos of this lovely text, and I'm grateful we've located it, and it appears unharmed. I'll notify the king that we've not only recovered his precious artifact but that we've revealed who stole it and will make sure she sees justice."

Bailey moaned, sinking into a chair and holding her face in her palms.

I wanted to go to her and hold her, to tell her everything would be alright, but I had to deal with this ass first.

"You two are having some sort of illicit relationship, and I'm sure you'll do anything to protect her, but there's no way you can brush this aside." Detective Carter actually stomped his boot on the floor.

I did the same, and he paused, staring at my boot.

"Frankly, Ms. Everhard, I'm gravely disappointed," he said, turning to my mate and approaching her. Because he was speaking gently and walking softly, I watched. If he touched her, I'd wrench him away and fling him against the wall. "To think you came highly recommended by the board. Ms. Merryweather spoke so well of you before she died. You were the obvious choice for the job." He stooped down in front of her, removing her hands from her face and placing them on her thighs.

I growled and stomped toward them to rip his arms off for touching her.

"Confess. Tell us why you took it, and we'll go easy on you. A year, maybe two in jail at the most, and you'll be free to go on with your life."

"I didn't steal the book!" She burst into tears and

leaped past him, rushing over to stand in front of me. "You know I didn't do it. You were with me this morning. The book wasn't here, and you knew where I was at all times today. There was no time when I could've returned home and placed the book there. Though why I'd steal it and leave it in plain view is beyond me."

"People do stupid things." Pure slime came through in the detective's voice as he joined us. It was all I could do not to wrap my fingers around his throat and squeeze.

My uncle would not approve of those methods. We had a treaty. These were the only reasons I held myself in check.

"You're a librarian," the detective said in a lulling voice. "I get it. Sometimes, people do bad things and often, they're not even sure why they did it. Impulse, maybe? You need money, I'm sure." He looked around her house as if assessing the worth of each item. "I imagine you had someone lined up to buy the book. If the traffic mishap hadn't happened, the book would probably already be on its way to its new home with none of us aware." His gaze met mine. "I'm sure you felt you had no choice. Do you need the money badly? Drugs maybe? Online gambling?"

"None of this is true." Bailey sent me a pleading look that made me want to sweep her up and take her to a place where no one could ever hurt her again. She didn't deserve this. She'd done no wrong.

"There's only one problem here," I said, tugging her against my side. My mate trembled, and I wanted to rip through this world and destroy it, starting with one particular detective. "Well, many problems actually, but we'll focus on one. This isn't the real book." I tossed it back onto the table.

Both Bailey and the detective gasped.

The detective lifted it and scrolled through the pages. "I assure you it is."

"And I assure *you*, that I, an expert on orc paper production, am confident that this," I poked the book, "is," I gouged it again, "not the real book."

"Of course it is," the detective blustered. "Look, I know you two are . . . mixed up in this together for whatever reason—"

"I love her." I said it softly, but the words were full of heart.

She gazed up at me with so much adoration in her eyes, I wanted to carry her to the bedroom and show her —with or without handcuffs. "I love you too, Katar."

"Mate." I turned her in my arms and cupped her face gently, giving her a kiss that contained a promise.

The detective grunted. "All this is beside the point. You can't prove this isn't the real book."

"I can," I said, giving the love of my life a grin. "The book you're holding may look like the real thing, but the paper didn't come from a frostmire tree."

"What's a frostmire tree?" he asked, frowning.

"Frostmire trees have a bluish tinge to the pulp that can be seen in the paper. Since the trees are nearly extinct, no one has used the trees for paper production for many generations. But long ago, it was considered the best tree to use for books of vital importance, which the ancient manuscript is." It was one of the oldest books in the orc collection and its theft had struck the very heart of orc culture. We had to find it, but this was not the original.

I took the book from him and sent Bailey a reassuring smile. We had to talk, figure out where we were going from here, because we were going to be together forever. There was no other future in store for us.

Flipping through the pages, I found one that had been torn and turned the book toward the detective, pointing at the side of the tear. "See right there? Not a hint of blue. Whoever made this forgery did an amazing job. If I didn't know about the special qualities of frost-mire, I'd be convinced myself this was the real book. But it isn't." I tossed it onto the table once more.

"Someone made a fake and planted it here to impli-cate me." Bailey shuddered and sunk onto the sofa. "Who would do such a thing?"

"You do realize I'll be verifying this frostmire theory," the detective said. "I'm not taking your word for it."

"Go ahead." I sat with her and tugged her onto my lap, holding her while she trembled. "We'll wait here for you to do the research you should've done already, then return to give Ms. Everhard an apology."

"I advise you not to leave town, Ms. Everhard," Detec-tive Carter said, scowling. "I'm not convinced of anything yet except that this appears to be the original manuscript."

I huffed. "The king would be horribly insulted if you sent that to him and insisted it was real. And believe me, you don't want to insult my uncle. He has a way of . . . *ruining* someone if they make such a grave mistake."

"Are you suggesting the king would make threats on my person?" He tugged on his jacket.

"I'd never say any such thing. But we have a treaty that outlines protocols for situations like this, although I doubt ancient texts and fakes are mentioned. I guess they should be."

"I reiterate once more. Do not leave town," the detective barked. He strode to the door and swung it open. "I'll return promptly as soon as I've verified what this orc has said." With that, he stomped outside and banged the door shut behind him.

Bailey slumped in my arms before she burst to her feet, looking around frantically. "Mozzie. Mozzie! Where are you, pup?"

31

BAILEY

I called Vera, who'd come over earlier to let Mozzie out into the backyard, but she didn't pick up. Braving the storm, Katar and I raced to Carole's house and knocked on her door.

She opened it, yawning while peering at both of us. "Bailey?" Her gaze took in Katar. "What's up?"

"Have you seen Mozzie?" Sometimes, he'd wander into her backyard, and she'd let him in. She kept chopped liver in her fridge to give him as a treat.

She stilled, and her frantic gaze shot to my house. "No, no, he isn't here."

I shook my head. "He's not at home, and I don't know how long he's been gone. The detective came, and I was distracted and didn't notice he wasn't there earlier."

"Detective?"

"He was waving handcuffs around and insisting he was going to arrest me and—"

"Arrest you for what?" She grabbed my hand and tugged me inside her gorgeous kitchen.

Katar followed us inside, shutting the door. He remained on the mat, looking around.

"Sit." Carole urged me into one of her mahogany bar stools. She poured me a glass of wine and nudged it toward me. "Drink. Breathe." Holding up the bottle, she tilted her head toward Katar.

"No thank you," he said, remaining where he was.

I sipped and placed the glass on the gleaming countertop.

Carole leaned her forearms on it and stared at me intently. "Tell me what's going on." I explained and her face filled with concern. "This makes no sense. Of course you didn't steal the book. Someone did, and I bet it's in a private collection by now."

"That's what I assume," I said with a sigh. "I don't know what to do."

"You're innocent. I'll call the detective and chew him out, tell him to leave you alone."

I appreciated that she'd speak up for me.

"As for Mozzie, you need to call the detective and tell him to investigate that instead." Her face crumpled. "I bet whoever left that fake book in your house took him or he got out somehow. Poor old guy." She rushed to her back window and peered out. "It's still raining. Cold. You've got to find him."

After taking another sip of wine, I rose and walked to the back door. "You're right. I need to call the detective."

"Keep me updated." Carole walked over and gave me a big hug. I was so grateful to have her as a friend. "Let me know if you find him. Please?"

I nodded and we left, returning home.

Collapsing on the sofa, I started to sob. "Mozzie. Mozzie."

"Let me go look around the neighborhood," Katar said. "Maybe he's hiding nearby, underneath a bush. He knows me. He'll come to my call."

"And if you don't find him?" My poor little pup. He was old. He needed me as much as I did him.

"We're going to find him. I promise."

32

KATAR

I didn't find Mozzie or any sign he'd been around Bailey's house. I hated returning home without her dog, but there wasn't anything else I could do. I placed a call to the detective, but he didn't sound very concerned about a missing pet. He did, however, state he'd look into it first thing in the morning. In between, he told me to call the local shelter and see if Mozzie had been turned in there.

He hadn't been. It was like the pup had disappeared off the face of the Earth.

In bed that night, I held Bailey while she cried. Neither of us slept well, and after checking in with both the detective and the shelter in the morning without any news, we went to the library.

"You should stay home," I said as she unlocked the front door.

"I can't. The community needs me." With the words stiffening her spine, she went inside and turned on the lights, getting ready for the first patrons to arrive.

I did some more investigating, but I didn't discover anything new.

When Vera arrived, Bailey rushed over to her.

"I tried to call you all last night, but you didn't pick up," Bailey said, frantic.

"I shut my phone off. I kept getting prank calls. I'm sorry. Did you need me?"

"Last night, when you put Mozzie outside, did you notice anything unusual at my house?"

Vera frowned as she hung her coat on a peg by the front door and turned to face us. "No. I let him out as usual, toweled off the dew because he was wet when I brought him in. I gave him a treat before locking up and leaving the key in the fake rock by the back steps. Is everything okay?"

"Mozzie's gone."

"No." Vera collapsed against the wall, stark fear widening her eyes. "Where could he be?"

"He hasn't come back, and no one has seen him." Bailey stretched out her hand, and I took it, giving it a squeeze off reassurance. "Detective Carter's looking for him and I've notified the shelter, but we can't find him anywhere."

"Aw, this is horrible." Vera hugged Bailey and the two women cried together.

"After I'm done today, I'll walk around your neighborhood, looking for him," Vera said. "He's got to be somewhere, and we'll find him."

"Thank you. I really appreciate it."

A woman and three children entered the library.

Vera stared after them as they walked into the big

front room. "I'll go sit at the desk in case they need anything, but please, let me know if you hear anything about Mozzie."

"I will," Bailey said.

We went to her office to strategize, but we didn't have any avenues we hadn't explored already.

After lunch and with Vera still working out front, we went back to the attic to do a further inventory with the list she'd printed in her office. Thankfully, she'd backed up her laptop and could access what she needed online.

We went through everything, carefully repacking the items in boxes, labeling them, and sealing them shut.

"I can't imagine why anyone bothered to go through old books," Bailey said, lifting the last one off the floor. "It's a lovely copy but not of any value except to someone who hoards old books like me." She gently placed it inside the box.

"Why do you keep them here?"

"I go through the stacks a few times a year and remove books based on how often they're checked out. If one is popular but our copy is getting worn, we replace it if we have the funds." She gave me a rueful smile. "I should throw them out, but I can't. You know? They're a part of history, but it's not just that. I feel like they're treasured friends and tossing them into the trash feels wrong. Vera said we should have a yard sale and sell them, and I think she's right. I've been packing them away up here with that in mind."

"Books can take you almost anywhere. They're an adventure, an escape. I understand." Taking her hand, I tugged her close and held her. "This is just one more reason why I love you. We haven't talked more about where this is going between us, but we will. Once all this is settled and we have Mozzie back, we'll sit down and figure it out."

"I'm willing to consider moving to the orc kingdom if orcs accept dogs." Her voice clogged with tears, and she sniffed. "Would he be welcome in the orc kingdom too?"

"Definitely. We love pets."

"Then after this is settled and Mozzie's back, which he will be," her voice grew in strength, "let's talk about visiting the orc kingdom. I've got some vacation time stored up, and I'm going to use it. Two weeks? Three? We'll decide. I want to see everything. All the places you love, and I want to try all the food. We'll explore, and we'll pick the best place for us both."

I'd never find another woman like Bailey. "Mate." I kissed her, and it tasted sweet. We were sharing our sorrow, the things we enjoyed and our hopes for the future. Nothing could taste better than that.

"Why don't we bring these boxes down to the hall outside my office?" she said after slipping away. "They've been up here too long already. Some were placed here by Helga herself. I'll get Vera and Carole busy organizing a yard sale, and we'll find new homes for each book with someone who'll love them as much as me."

"I'll be happy to carry them down for you."

She lifted one and gave me a smile. "We'll do it together."

There were a lot of boxes in the attic, and it took us an hour to bring most of them down. We stacked them along one side of the back hall, and the pile soon grew almost high enough to touch the ceiling.

"Why didn't Helga have me do this ages ago?" Bailey asked. Back in the attic, she'd paused before lifting the top box off the final pile and was rubbing her lower back.

I went over and did it for her, and she was soon moaning and wiggling beneath my touch.

"Let's continue this later," she said with a growl. "You can massage me, and I'll do the same for you."

I pressed her up against the wall and soon lost myself in her mouth, the way she arched her spine to reach my touch.

"Anyone up there?" a voice called out from the bottom of the stairs.

I lifted my head and Bailey gave me a dreamy look.

"Hello?" they called again.

Bailey's eyes widened. She scooted underneath my arm. "I'm coming, Vera." She turned back at the top of the stairs. "I'll be back in a sec to help you carry down the rest of the boxes."

"I'll do it. You go see what Vera needs and then sit. You've worked hard enough already."

"Thank you. I'll call the shelter and the detective to see if they've heard anything about Mozzie."

She hurried down the stairs and soon her and Vera's voices echoed up to me. Something about a patron wanting to order a series of books and Vera being unsure how to find them on the computer.

I carried more boxes downstairs.

I was bending forward to lift the last one when something odd on the wall drew my attention.

A door?

"Maybe it leads to another attic room," I whispered, outlining the panel with my fingertips.

I carried the last box downstairs and placed it with the others, then hunted down Bailey who was sitting at the computer out front, showing Vera more ways to find books. When I approached, Vera rose and rushed over to take a water bottle away from a teenager who'd just entered through the front door.

"We can't have drinks in the library," she said, though kindly.

"Did you know there was a door behind the stack of boxes?" I asked Bailey.

She looked up at me, frowning. "No. Are you sure?"

"A door?" Vera asked, and I nodded.

"Come see," I said to Bailey, taking her hand.

"We'll be right back, Vera."

Still frowning, Vera nodded again.

We returned upstairs.

"This is so weird," Bailey said, staring at the door. She reached out and lifted the antique latch, but the panel wouldn't open. "It seems to be stuck."

"Want me to try?"

When she stepped back, I wiggled the panel, and something clicked. I lifted the latch, and it opened easily.

Stepping through it, we found a dusty staircase leading down.

33

BAILEY

"I can't believe this is here," I exclaimed. "Let me grab a flashlight and we can investigate." I raced to my office, only stopping in the front room to let Vera know I might be a few more minutes.

"What's up with the door?" she asked, shooting a look in that direction.

"It was hidden behind the pile of boxes," I gushed with excitement. "Did you know it was where?"

"No," she breathed. "A door to where?"

"No idea. We're going to—"

A teenager came up to the desk, and while Vera was taking care of his requestion, I returned upstairs and switched on the light, handing it to Katar.

"This is your library, sweetheart," he said.

"And you found the door. I can't believe I didn't know it was here all this time. I wonder why Helga didn't mention it. She must've known about it."

"Is there a plan of the building?"

"Only one showing the location of fire exits. There's

no second set of stairs on the map." I grinned his way. "You go first."

"You're sure?" At my nod, Katar took the flashlight from me and stepped through the opening to the other side. He flashed the light around, grunting, but didn't say anything. When he started down the stairs, I followed. Worn and cracked, the boards creaked under our feet.

"Do you think this is safe?" I whispered.

"Seems to be." He reached a landing and started down another level. "The stairs appear to go to the basement."

"The basement is as old as the library, which was built in the 1800s. The basement walls are made up of big slabs of granite and you saw the dirt floor, the cobwebs, the equally ancient boiler. It wouldn't surprise me if a body was buried down there ages ago. It . . . smells." And that was a creepy thought. Goosebumps peppered my skin. "I can't imagine why no one has mentioned this stairwell to me. Surely, someone on the board knows about it."

"Or the person who stole the orc manuscript and trashed your attic and office. They were looking for something, and I suspect this is how they got inside without being seen on the cameras."

"They'd still need to leave the basement." I frowned. "But if they stayed there until the library was busy, no one would notice them coming or going. It really is all connected."

"I believe so."

We reached the bottom of the stairs and found an arched tunnel leading to the right plus a door on the left.

Katar cracked the door open, but it would only budge about six inches until he shifted aside a bunch of dusty paint cans.

"This is the closet under the other basement stairs," I whispered, still feeling too scared to speak in a normal tone.

When the passage was clear, we walked into the basement but didn't see anything unusual. I couldn't tell if anyone had remained in the basement for hours, but they'd probably make sure there was no evidence left behind.

"Let's check out the tunnel," I said, returning to the newly discovered staircase. I squinted but couldn't see far in the dark. "I wonder where it leads."

"Let's find out." Taking my hand, he stepped forward, the flashlight guiding our way as we walked crouched over to keep from hitting our heads on the low stone ceiling.

"It smells like the woods after it rains," I whispered. "Crushed leaves and vegetation."

Katar grunted.

After we walked a few hundred yards, we came to yet another door. It opened out on the side of a hill in the woods behind the library.

Katar nodded as he looked around but there was no one near and all I heard was the rustle of squirrels and a few birds chirping.

He grunted. "This must be how someone got inside the library without the cameras picking them up."

One clue. Would it lead us to whoever had stolen the book?

34

KATAR

"We need to call Detective Carter," Bailey said as we took the tunnel and stairs back to the attic, closing all the doors after passing through them.

"Let's hold off on that." I nudged my head to the door in the attic wall. "Don't tell anyone what we've found. Not yet."

"But it will help clear my name."

"He seems pretty determined to pin this on you. Have you ever considered why?"

She sucked in a breath. "Do you think he could be involved?"

"Hard to say but he's definitely a suspect."

"What are we going to do?" She hugged her arms around her waist and shivered.

I held her until she stopped shaking.

"We'll look around some more," I said, ideas already springing up in my mind. "And when we've finished and if we decide he's not involved, we'll fill him in on what we've found." This was where it mattered that the king had put me in charge of the investigation. If the detective had his say, the case would be closed already.

We went back downstairs and returned the flashlight to my office.

"Ah, there you are," Vera said with a smile, walking in right as we were putting it away. "Tell me what's going on! I've been dying to find out."

Bailey's gaze met mine and she shook her head. "The door didn't go anywhere. Just . . . to another side of the attic."

"Aw," Vera said. "That's disappointing. I thought we had a budding mystery in the library, and we could all be sleuths."

"Not this time."

I could tell by the look in her eyes that Bailey didn't like keeping this from Vera, but everyone was a suspect.

"Well, back to my regular old boring life. At least I have a cat." Vera laughed. "It's four and time for me to leave, but I'm on the schedule for tomorrow morning. I was wondering if I could come in late. I've got a few errands to run and most of the places aren't open until nine."

"Of course," Bailey said. "You know we're flexible."

"Thank you. I'm going to drive over to your place right now and start looking for Mozzie." She held up her phone. "If I see anything or find him, I'll let you know right away."

"Thank you." Bailey sent me a teary look. "I'm worried about him."

"Me, too. I can't imagine where he must've gone."

Vera left, and we went out front, Bailey sitting at the

desk to help patrons while I strolled around the library, thinking. I didn't come to any conclusions by the time we'd left, though I had plenty of avenues I wanted to explore in the morning. I'd start with the woods tomorrow during daylight hours.

We went to Bailey's house and went inside.

"I want to look around for Mozzie too," she said, gnawing on her lower lip. "I know Vera's looking but maybe he won't come to her call."

We put on jackets and scoured the area, walking in widening circles, but we found no sign of her pup.

Returning home, we collapsed on the sofa.

That's when we found the envelope on the table with Bailey's name written in block letters. After shooting a shocked look my way, she opened it and pulled out the very brief message.

Be at the park at six tomorrow evening.
Bring the book.
If you go to the cops, I'll hurt the dog.

35

BAILEY

"I don't know what this means," I cried after studying the simple map and throwing the letter onto the coffee table. I pressed my back against the couch. "*What* book? I've got to figure this out. They've got Mozzie, and they're going to hurt him."

Katar gently held my face, stroking away my tears with his thumb. "It's going to be alright. We'll get Mozzie back. At least we know where he is."

"I hope they're not hurting him. He's such a sweet guy, but he's old. His heart can't take much stress."

He growled. "I'll fix this for you."

"I'm so glad you're here with me." I stared at the note. "Should we quietly notify the detective? This is more evidence, perhaps enough to at least convince him I'm not involved with the theft of the book."

"Let's think for a moment."

"Do you think it's one of the books Helga gave me? They can have them all as long as they give back Mozzie, safe and sound."

His head tilted and he frowned, seeming to stare inward. "Would you do something for me?"

"Sure."

"Open your birthday book gift from Helga."

"I can't right now. I'm too stressed about Mozzie."

"I think . . ." He huffed. "It's an odd thought, but I wonder . . ."

"I can get it. There's no harm in opening it now, I guess." I went to my room and tugged the box where I'd placed it out from underneath my bed, dragging a few dust bunnies out along with it. The box was labeled old clothes, and I'd carefully placed the gift there to keep it out of Mozzie's reach. He might be an old dog, but he still occasionally enjoyed chewing, especially cardboard, for whatever reason. I didn't want to risk the gift.

Taking it to the living room, I joined Katar on the couch again and placed the box on my lap. After tracing my name scrolled on the front of the box, I slit the tape with scissors and opened it. Inside, I found what looked like another first edition wrapped in the same special paper she'd always used. It hurt to see it, to know this was the last time I'd open a birthday present from her.

After brushing aside a few tears, I set the box on the sofa and carefully unwrapped the gift on my lap. My stunned silence rang out when I saw what was hidden behind the pretty paper.

"It's . . ." I couldn't quite believe it and when I turned it gently onto its side and examined the paper, I knew from the hint of blue. "It's the original orc manuscript. But . . . how did it wind up here?"

Katar pulled an envelope out from among the wrapping paper and handed it to me. It had my name on it. "Perhaps this will give you an answer."

Opening it, I pulled out a note.

Dearest Bailey,

Your last gift! I'm so sorry I won't be there to get your thoughts about the enclosed book. I did so much enjoy hearing the joy in your voice when you gushed about my latest gift.

I've asked my lawyer to send this to you in time for your birthday. Open it and think of me and know I'm smiling down on you from somewhere above.

You're going to find this strange. I did a naughty thing. Shhh... After we locked the original orc text under the glass cabinet, I often found one particular person snooping. One time, I could swear they were trying to pry open the case! I couldn't prove anything, so I decided to watch them.

I also wanted to make sure that, if they got the case open, they wouldn't touch the precious book.

I was worried and you know me, I always trust my instincts.

It's surprising what a person can do online if they put their mind to it. I had a fake copy of the book made and put it inside the case. Then I hid the original. My plan was to destroy the fake when it was time to return the original book to the orc kingdom. Naturally, I'd only send the proper copy back to the king. But I got sick, and I didn't know what to do.

Bailey, I thought. Bailey will handle this in the proper manner.

So, here it is. You probably haven't even discovered there's a fake book under the glass case, and that makes me chuckle.

Take a peek at the original before you decide what to do. I know you were itching to get your hands on it when it arrived, but the orcs weren't keen on letting anyone touch it. After that, hide it in a secure place and finish my plan.

No one will ever know the original hasn't been inside the glass case the entire time.

Your dear friend,

Helga

I sucked in a breath and let it gush out of me before looking up at Katar. "Now we know what book the person wants in exchange for Mozzie."

36

KATAR

We worked out a plan and Bailey called some volunteers to cover the library the next day, saying she was sick and couldn't go in.

We prepared everything early, trying to make sure we'd covered every angle and possibility.

I ran to the park hours before the meet-up time. I wanted to be in place well ahead of the person. I was eager to get this over with. I was going to protect my mate, make sure her pet was safely back in her arms, and bring the real villain to justice. Orc justice, that is. Per the treaty, crimes committed against the orc kingdom would be prosecuted there, not here under human law.

Crouched down behind a long row of bushes, I watched the location where Bailey was supposed to meet the person. She'd drive to the park closer to the set time.

As the sun sunk toward the horizon, I sat quietly, waiting.

Bailey arrived and finding no one there, sat on a park bench, the book on her lap inside a tote bag.

We waited.

I remained still, determined to end this tonight. Bailey shifted on the bench, clearly worried about Mozzie.

Finally, about twenty minutes after the set time, someone wearing a motorcycle helmet with a dark visor pulled down and a leather biker outfit strolled over to this section of the park, their black boots nearly silent on the grass. Mozzie was not with them.

They strode right up to Bailey. I studied them, trying to determine who it might be. They were tall, but from the loose leathers, I couldn't tell if the person was male or female.

"Give me the book," they growled in a low voice that gave nothing away.

Bailey rose, clutching the book to her chest. "Where's Mozzie?"

"In a safe place."

Bailey lifted her chin. "You can't have the book until you give him back to me."

"Give me the book!"

"No." Bailey stepped backward and put the park bench between her and the person.

When they raced after her, I'd had enough. With a roar, I leaped over the long row of bushes and across the open area, tackling the person to the ground. They struggled, but no one could take down an orc determined to protect his mate.

Bailey raced over and lifted the motorcycle visor, gasping at who she found. "Carole?"

Carole snarled.

I sat her up, tying her wrists behind her back and securing her ankles with the cuffs the detective had so nicely given to me. As a double measure, I secured the cuffs to one of the stone park bench's legs. She couldn't get away now.

"Give me the book and your dog will survive," she growled, not looking at me.

I tightened my grip on Carole's upper arm, glaring down at her. "Where is Mozzie?"

She smirked. "Where you'll never find him now."

"The cops are coming," Bailey said. "They're going to arrest you, and you're going to jail—orc jail."

Carole's smirk wavered. "What do you mean by that? Even if you can prove I was somehow involved in . . . dognapping, I guess one might call this, I don't believe any other crime has been committed. You've got nothing on me that will result in more than a slap on the wrist."

"You stole the orc manuscript," Bailey said. "You broke into the library from the wooded entrance and made your way through the tunnel. You rummaged through the attic, my office, and my house. You were looking for the book. Somehow, you knew Helga had given it to me."

She grinned at Bailey. "Even if I admitted I'd done all that, which I'm not, it's nothing. I doubt I'd even get community service."

"You're forgetting that you won't be tried here on the surface," I said with complete satisfaction. "In the orc kingdom, we take the wellbeing of our pets quite seriously. Causing them harm, and stress is harm for any dog, let alone one as old as Mozzie, is punished with ten years of hard labor in the kingdom's mines." I hauled her to her feet.

She tried to kick me. "Let me go." Her helmet tilted, and I pulled it off, tossing it aside. "Okay, so I did it. I stole the book, then discovered it wasn't the real deal. I then tried to find it, but I had no idea where you'd hidden it." Her glare shot Bailey's way. "Then I remembered Helga gave you books all the time. She must've snuck the real one out and substituted it with a fake. I figured you'd know where the original was."

"And I kidnapped your stupid pup," she said. "He whined in my garage all night long. But it's your word against mine, and I'm not saying a thing to an orc judge."

"Mozzie's in her garage," Bailey breathed, her voice full of excitement. "He's safe."

Carole huffed. "I don't hurt dogs."

"Why?" Bailey asked. "Why would you tell me that? You don't need the book."

"My trust fund's getting low and, well, I don't like to scrimp. I planned to sell the original book for a lot of money."

"And now you won't." Detective Carter stepped out from behind the bushes where I'd waited. He nodded to both Bailey and me. "I appreciate the help, Katar, but I can take it from here. She'll be arraigned and remanded to the orc kingdom where she'll stand before the king and state her case." He untied the binding securing her to the park bench, then started leading her toward the entrance to the park.

"I get a trial," Carole shouted, hobbling beside him.

"No trial," I called after her. "We'll tell the king what

you did, and he'll hand down the sentence. That's how justice is handled in the orc kingdom."

"No . . ." she wailed as the detective led her away.

I held out my arms, and Bailey rushed over and jumped into them.

"We'll go rescue Mozzie from Carole's place," she said between kisses. "And we'll bring him home and give him lots of treats and snuggles and tell him what a good boy he is. And then . . ."

"Then?" I grinned down at her, grateful it was over, and Mozzie would soon be safe.

She latched onto my horns and gave me a heady kiss before easing away to grin at me. "And then we need to go wild."

37

EPILOGUE 1

BAILEY

Six Months Later

"Very well, Your Majesty." I bowed to the orc king and strode through his receiving room, my heels clicking on the marble flooring, and my skirt swirling around my calves.

As we walked, Katar squeezed my hand and leaned close to whisper. "That went well."

I shot him a smile and nodded, waiting to speak until after we'd left the receiving room. I was a wreck. Yes, I'd prepared my presentation and practiced it a billion times, and Katar had helped where he could, but I wasn't sure what the king would think about my idea.

Outside the receiving room, I collapsed on an orc-sized bench, my feet dangling in the air. Katar joined me, lifting me and placing me on his lap with my legs wrapping around his waist.

My orcling bump took up the area between our bellies. I was due in four months.

"The king said yes," I crowed up at Katar. "Yes!"

Katar's arms tightened around me. "I knew he would."

"You said that, and I tried to hold faith, but, well, I'm glad that part of the plan is over." I stiffened my spine like Helga Merryweather used to do when someone acted unruly in the library's front room. "You're now looking at the new head librarian of the king's private book collection on the surface. He's going to let me put them on display and let sociologists study them. Under my strict eye, however." She winked. "And with my own private investigator on hand, no one will dare touch the collection."

One might think the book collection was fifteen, maybe twenty books, but no. This king enjoyed old books almost as much as me, and he'd had a special building built to house them. It had three floors of stacks and more sliding ladders than the library back home.

My true home was wherever I could be with Katar, but we'd had a long talk after everything was wrapped up related to the ancient text. Katar wanted to open a PI business and hire other monsters, and I was eager to curate my own special collection. I'd given up my job at the library, but I planned to volunteer.

Vera had stepped into my shoes as head librarian and was doing an amazing job. She'd run an auction for the old books, making sure each one went to the right person, and she'd raised some money doing it.

I'd help her out whenever I could.

While the guards standing on either side of the enormous doors tried not to look like they were watching us instead of the long room in front of them, I curled my finger toward my mate. I couldn't wait to go to our temporary home in the hills, a large estate the king had given us as a mating present, and drag my love off to our bedroom.

We'd spend our vacation time here in the future.

I had a thing for Katar's horns and . . . well, you know.

We kissed, and it soon grew steamy inside the anteroom, so I eased away from his delicious mouth.

"Later, mate?" I said with a smile. "I've got some new ideas for how I can go wild." We'd become quite inventive when it came to setting my inner Bailey free, and we often challenged each other to surprise the other with something new.

"Maybe not later?" he growled, standing with me in his arms.

I wiggled my eyebrows. "I'm listening."

He leaned near my ear. "Care to strip everything off and run through the receiving room? We can meet up at the throne."

I smacked his arm, though gently. "You. Stop teasing me. We can't do that."

His lips curled around his tusks with his smile. "Who says I'm teasing?"

"We'd get into trouble."

Now, the guards really were listening in. The mouth of the one on the right had dropped open.

"I happen to know the king planned to leave the receiving room after your meeting," Katar said. "There's no one there, and you said you always wanted to sit on a throne. I thought, since you were sitting there, you could settle on me." He tugged something out of his back pocket and dangled handcuffs in front of my face. "And after, I thought we could try these out."

OMG, yessss. I pressed my face against his chest, speaking only for him. "We've got to do this, but how?"

"There's the mate I adore. As for that . . ." He gently lowered me to the floor and went over to speak with the guards.

They nodded and left.

Then Katar and I started ripping off our clothing.

38

EPILOGUE 2
KATAR

Two Months Later

I sat in my new office in my newly opened business, Monsters, PI, with my feet up on my desk and my newest hire, a former gargoyle government agent sitting in the chair across from my desk. Because I'd hired a gargoyle as my first employee, and I was interviewing an ice lord in a few weeks for my open position, I'd purposefully bought furniture that fit monsters.

It also went with my business's name.

We'd barely hung the shingle outside before the phone started ringing. While we'd yet to be hired for a big case, we'd handled missing pets, tracking down the furry escapees. A week ago, we'd located the local high school's class of 2002's time capsule, then hung around to help them excavate it fully and exclaim about the contents. We'd even been hired to track down a missing gromgret mascot costume, finally locating it in the woods behind the high school. A moose had somehow snagged it on its rack and took off with it. It fell off about three miles from the school.

We'd taken on numerous challenges thus far.

These jobs might not generate much income, but it was a start. I had enough wealth to support my new business for a very long time. Solid cases would come in soon. We knew it.

"How are you doing with the garden gnome kidnapping case?" I asked Tuvid.

He shifted in the chair, adjusting his closed wings, and for some reason, his deep blue skin darkened. "The case has been solved. I discovered who was stealing the poor little buggers."

Humans might think garden gnomes were merely stone statues, but not so. They lived and thrived as much as the rest of us monsters.

"How did you crack the case?"

"I set up trail cams near every remaining garden gnome in the vicinity," he said. "And last night, I picked up some footage. I got a license plate that led me to the guy's home. When he let me inside his home to ask questions, I heard the gnomes squealing."

Tuvid had exceptional hearing, something that came in handy while working a job like this.

"He confessed, I waited with him until the local detective arrived, and then I returned the gnomes to the homes they were stolen from."

I nodded slowly. "Perfect. Is there anything else we should discuss?"

Before he could speak, Bailey tapped on my office door and tucked her head through the opening. She'd offered to do her job while sitting at the reception desk until we could hire someone. Like with the ice lord, I had some potential prospects with interviews lined up, something I'd take care of when we got back from our vacation.

"You've got a case," she said with a big grin. "A good one too."

"All of our cases are good," I said with a grin, taking in her gorgeous face and her body swelling with our orcling. She'd deliver in about three months, and I couldn't wait.

"You know what I mean."

Rising, I went over to tug her inside. If Tuvid wasn't here, I'd shut the door, lift her up, and press her against the wall. Or sweep everything off my desk and lay her back on the surface. Sadly, with Tuvid around, all I could do was give her a sweet kiss.

"Let me guess," I said after. "More background checks for the new dating service in town?"

"Not yet, though I imagine Bettina will have plenty of those soon." She leaned against the back of the door. "Angie Granger's here."

Tuvid jolted in his chair. Did he know her?

"The owner of the local microbrewery, Beastly Brews?" Bailey and I had plans to go to a tasting there soon. I didn't drink much beer, but what I'd sipped, I'd enjoyed. I planned to buy some of their specialty brews while I was there. Support a local business and all that.

"She's got a case for you!"

Tuvid rose and turned to lean against the side of his

chair. He was as tall and equally broad as me, though there was a sharpness to his face that told anyone who met him that this male didn't fool around. He'd come highly recommended. Frankly, he had more experience than what a small-town business like this needed, but during his interview, he'd quietly told me he was eager for a change. He'd finished a tough case involving statue theft in Europe and wanted to work on simpler cases.

Monsters, PI was exactly what he was looking for, and I was grateful to have him on my staff.

"What's Angie's problem?" he asked in a deadly voice. Bailey once told me she found his voice smooth and silky. I couldn't tell, but then, I wasn't female. To me, Tuvid was a decent guy and a smart investigator. He talked like everyone else I knew. Who cared if he had a nice ass— something else Bailey had pointed out.

"Mystic Harbor is hosting a brew-off where area microbreweries will compete for a cash prize, plus a featured spot in the Monster Beer Blog," Bailey said. "They went viral a while ago and have fantastic reach. The post is sure to make a bestseller out of the winner. Angie planned to enter her new beer, a chocolate chili pepper stout, in the event, but the kegs have gone missing from her locked storage."

The event would be held in a week. No brew meant no prize or potential buzz for her business. I could only imagine how upset she was.

"She spoke with Detective Carter, and he conducted an investigation," Bailey rolled her eyes. "He's found no clues. That's when she decided to come to us."

"You'll need to handle this one," I told Tuvid. "Since

Bailey and I will be on vacation for the next week." We were traveling to the orc kingdom to visit the king and watch a few gromgret games.

Tuvid swallowed hard and gave me a curt nod. I could swear he'd lost some of his color, though I had no idea why. This agent never flinched at anything.

"I'll bring her into your office," Bailey told Tuvid, backing from the room.

We moved over to Tuvid's office, and he settled in his chair while I leaned against the wall. I'd hang out in case he needed my input, but otherwise, I'd only listen out of curiosity.

Bailey opened the door and stepped inside, leading a curvy woman with thick, curly blonde hair.

"You," the woman snarled.

"Um, yes, me," he croaked, rising from his chair.

"Do you two know each other?" Bailey asked.

"Yes," Tuvid said.

"No," Angie shouted.

With a shake of her head, Bailey made the introductions. "Angie Granger, this is Tuvid Elresh, who, I guess, you already know. Angie's the owner of the microbrewery in need of our services."

Angie snarled. She raced around Tuvid's desk and stood in front of him, her fists on her hips and her freckled cheeks florid. "Not from you."

"Angie," he said, jumping to his feet. "Um, yeah."

Bailey and I looked at each other with raised eyebrows—brow ridge in my case—and it was clear neither of us knew what to do.

Angie poked Tuvid's chest. "This man accused me of

theft." She whirled around to face me and my mate. "Assign another agent."

"We can't," Bailey said. "Katar and I are leaving town tomorrow, and we won't be back for ten days." She gave me a weak smile. "We planned to leave town, that is."

"I can handle this," Tuvid said. "You two go ahead. I'll take down the information and help Angie."

"Are you alright with that?" I asked Angie.

"You're sure there's no one else available?" she asked.

"I've got some interviews lined up for when I come back, but for now, Tuvid is my only available agent."

She sighed. "Alright. We'll make this work."

I took Bailey's hand, and we backed out of the room, closing the door behind them.

Voices echoed inside, though more subdued now.

"Should we cancel our vacation?" Bailey asked. "Angie needs help and from what I just saw, she might not want Secret Agent Gargoyle Tuvid on the case."

Secret Agent was Bailey's new nickname for Tuvid. He found it funny and laughed whenever she said it.

"Let's give them a moment and then we'll ask," I said. "This could be our last chance to visit before our orcling arrives."

Things suddenly went silent inside the office.

"I'll take a peek." Bailey carefully turned the knob and cracked the door open. She ducked back out into the hall and leaned against the wall; her eyes wide. "I think we can go on vacation."

"Have they stopped arguing?"

"I believe so."

"Only believe?"

"He's holding her in his arms. His wings are wrapped around her." She frowned my way. "Too bad you don't have wings."

I huffed. "You don't like heights."

"That's not true."

"Then why wouldn't you open your eyes when we climbed to the top of that lighthouse?"

"Because . . . Because . . ."

I chuckled. "Gargoyles don't have tusks," I pointed out. "Tusks are better than fangs."

Her pretty cheeks darkened. Was she remembering what I'd done with my tusks last night?

Bailey sashayed over to me and traced her fingertip down the front of my shirt. "Tusks are better than fangs."

I wrapped my arms around her. "And my arms area a decent substitution for wings."

"They are." A shiver tracked through her, and she smiled up at me.

I tilted my head toward Tuvid's door. "Should I go in there and remind him we have rules about fraternizing with the clients?" Assuming that's what was going on right now.

"Do we really have that rule?"

I shrugged. "Maybe."

"Does the rule extend to staff fraternizing among *staff* as well?" She looked up at me with heat in her eyes.

"Absolutely not." I swept her up into my arms and bolted to my office.

Thankfully, I'd already installed a good lock.

I hope you enjoyed Katar and Bailey's story!
I had so much fun writing their romance and
infusing it with a touch of mystery.

Look for *Secret Agent Gargoyle* –
Tuvid & Angie's story,
the first book in my series, Monsters, PI

Pick up Rexin and Adeline's
story in Single Orc Dad.

And Cat & Dugar's romance in
Orc Charming
(a prequel novella in the
Love at First Orc Series that's FREE!)
**I'm falling for my gorgeous orc roommate,
but he's got a secret.**

Other Freebies for you:
Just sign up for my newsletter,
and I'll send them to you.

Orc's Mate
(a full-length story set in the Monster Mate Hunt Series)
On the night of the Monster Hunt,

I must run through the forest
—where an orc will claim me as his bride.

Escorting the Alien
(a prequel novella set in the Beastly Alien Boss Series)
I'm trapped on a volcanic planet with
a surly alien who thinks I'm his for the taking.
What could go wrong with that?

ABOUT THE AUTHOR

Ava Ross is a two-time *USA Today* Bestselling author who has written numerous titles, all of them featuring sweet and steamy romance. She fell for men with unusual features when she first watched Star Wars, where alien creatures have gone mainstream. She lives in New England with her husband (who is sadly not an alien, though he is still cute in his own way), her kids, and a few assorted pets.

ALSO BY AVA ROSS

Mail-Order Brides of Crakair

Brides of Driegon

Fated Mates of the Ferlaern Warriors

Fated Mates of the Xilan Warriors

Holiday with a Cu'zod Warrior

Galaxy Games

Alien Warrior Abandoned

Beastly Alien Boss

Bride of the Fae

A Sci-Fi Holiday Tail

Monsterville, USA

Monster on Board

(co-written with Alana Khan)

Love at First Orc

Monster Mate Hunt

Sweet Monster Treats

Brides of the Zuldrux Warriors

Single Titles

A Monster Worth Fighting For

Craving Stardust

Dad Bod Dragon

Mated to the Dragon

Jasmine's Grumpy Genie

Swamp Thing (You Make My Heart Sing)

You can find her books on Amazon.

SECRET AGENT GARGOYLE

**Do I dare trust my heart to
Secret Agent Gargoyle?**

Angie: When my specialty beer kegs turn up missing days before a big brew-off event, I hire Monsters, PI to track down my beer. Who's assigned to my case? Tuvid Elresh, the gargoyle who wrongfully accused me of gnome-theft a few short weeks ago.

Tuvid's seven feet of bulging gargoyle muscles with a killer—fang-filled—smile. So, when our *not*-one-night-stand inside a beer cooler results in a spontaneous proposal of marriage—solely to save his gargoyle rep—I know I'm in deep trouble. My business plans don't include marrying a gargoyle, but Tuvid's impossible to resist. Will I lose my heart to a gargoyle secret agent?

Tuvid: I met Angie while I was wrapping up a local investigation involving stolen gnomes. Yeah, I was given the wrong address, and I accused her of stealing the little guys. I was determined to make amends. Plus ask her out, because she's cute. But she didn't return my calls.

Then we're locked inside her microbrewery's cold storage, and who should unlock the door in the morning? Her mom and mine. It's clear we've been together all night, though we didn't do anything—well, not much. But gargoyles are old-fashioned, and my reputation will be shattered unless we get married.

I'm not a gargoyle who'll waste an opportunity like this. I'm going to track down her beer kegs in time for the brew-off. And when the case is closed? Angie's going to be my gargoyle bride.

Secret Agent Gargoyle is Book 1 in the Monsters, PI Series. It's a cute and steamy romance featuring a cinnamon roll gargoyle with creative body parts, on-the-page heat, size difference, a cozy mystery, lots of laughs, and a HEA guaranteed.

CHAPTER 1

ANGIE

The discreet sign mounted discreetly on the front of the building said, *Monsters, PI.* My destination.

After parking in the lot on Main Street in my cozy coastal town of Mystic Harbor, Massachusetts, I got out of my car. I waited for a vehicle to pass before hurrying across the road and entering the building. Monsters, PI had opened a few months ago and was run by Katar Dolkin, an orc who used to do undercover work. He'd solved the theft of an ancient book from our local library and fallen in love with the librarian along the way. Rather than return to the orc kingdom, he'd decided to remain in town and set up a new business.

Not long ago, monsters stepped out of the woodwork, more or less, or emerged from wherever they'd been hiding to join human society. Treaties were formed, and monsters took jobs. Bought property. And started dating humans.

Now it was pretty normal to see a yeti loping down the street with full shopping bags in hand or an ogre parking her truck in front of the new ice cream shop, Creature Cones.

I stepped inside Monsters, PI and walked over to where Bailey sat at the receptionist's desk. Not long ago, she ran our library. Now she was Katar's mate and the curator of an exclusive orc manuscript collection. I heard she was filling in here until they could hire a receptionist.

"Hey, Angie, how are you?" she asked, rising and coming around the desk to give me a quick hug.

"Not so good," I said.

"Ah." Bailey stepped back and leaned against the desk. "You didn't stop in to say hello, then."

"Unfortunately, no. Someone stole my potentially prize-winning kegs of stout from my microbrewery, Beastly Beer Co."

Mystic Harbor had gone all-in with the monster theme, changing business names to fit. Now you got your hair cut at Claws & Curls, you bought your hardware supplies at Shriek & Nail, and the Salty Fang Pub had all the local microbrews on tap—including three crafted at my business.

And those were just the names I could come up with off the top of my head.

"Who do you think stole your beer?" Bailey asked, cupping her cheeks with her palms.

"No idea. Detective Carter can't find any clues. That's why I came here. I thought Katar might take on the case."

"I know he'll be happy to help." She gazed toward the hall on her right, and I spied open office doors beyond. "Can you give me a few more details about the case before I go speak with Katar?"

"You must've heard of the Monster Mash Brew-off."

"It's all the people of this town can talk about. It's next Saturday, right?"

I nodded. "Yes. Everyone within a hundred-mile radius will descend on the local fairgrounds to sample beer from almost one hundred microbreweries. Not all at once, of course, but you know what I mean. They're holding a contest for the best brew, and the winner will receive a cash prize. The prize isn't the most exciting part about the event. Whoever wins will be featured on the Monster Beer Blog."

She frowned, tapping her pencil on her desk. "They went viral on TickingClock not long ago, didn't they?"

"Exactly, and whoever they feature has a great chance of going viral as well. The winner of Best Brew is sure to see tons of sales not long after that."

"You're entering a beer, aren't you?" she asked.

"I'd planned to, but that's why I'm here. My kegs of chocolate chili pepper stout, the recipe I've spent years perfecting, were stolen."

"No," Bailey breathed.

"It's horrible. I can't enter if I don't have that beer, which is why I came to Monsters, PI. Do you think Katar can help me track my kegs down in time for the brew-off?"

Male voices echoed from down the hall, and I recognized Katar's among them. The other voice spoke too low for me to make out more than a gruff tone.

For whatever reason, the sound of it sent tingles across my skin.

Yeah, I needed to start dating again so I could stop

dreaming about the snooty gargoyle detective who'd accused me of gnome theft. Hello? My gnomes weren't alive, though I now knew some were. I'd made mine in ceramics class, something I did to unwind after a long day at work.

When the gargoyle detective flew over my backyard and landed near my prized tulip bed, I thought he'd stopped by to tell me how amazing my gardens looked from above. While I smiled at him and he grinned at me, I'd taken in his tall, muscular frame. His killer, fanged smile. His gorgeous, deep blue wings.

Then he flashed his ID and gave me the impression he was about to haul me to the police station to be booked for gnome theft.

I'd told him in no uncertain terms I had not stolen my gnomes, and I showed him the receipt for he classes I'd taken that noted the five custom-painted figurines standing in my gardens. Then I waved to the sky and told him to fly away on the gust of wind he rode in on.

I hadn't seen or heard from him since.

"You came to the right place," Bailey said. "I bet Monsters, PI can track down your kegs."

"As soon as possible, please. Detective Carter said whoever did it didn't leave a single clue."

"We'll do all we can to track them down for you. Wait here, and I'll go speak to Katar. I'm sure he can squeeze you in for an appointment right now. If I know my orc mate's crew, they'll be tracking down clues in no time."

"Thank you." Tears bloomed in my eyes, and I fumbled for a tissue while Bailey left the reception area and strode down the hall, returning a few minutes later.

"You're in luck," she said, patting my arm. "Are you okay?"

"You know me. I cry quite easily." That was an understatement. Everyone around town knew my mom and I cried for almost no reason at all.

"We've recently hired a new agent," Bailey said. "And he's just wrapped up a big case and has time to take on yours. Come with me, and I'll introduce you to him. You can explain the situation, and he'll start looking into it right away."

"I really appreciate it." I followed her down the hall and into an office, where I nodded to Ketar leaning against the wall on my left before looking toward the big wooden desk placed in the back of the good-sized room, taking in the gargoyle sitting in the chair behind it.

"You!" I snarled, gaping at the guy I'd booted out of my backyard last week, the gorgeous gargoyle I'd crushed on for about three minutes before he accused me of gnome-theft.

He looked up, his dark gray eyes locking on me.

I sucked in a breath and . . . it remained frozen in my lungs. My heart turned solid along with it.

"Um, yes, me," he croaked.

"Do you two know each other?" Bailey asked, her smile fading.

"Yes," Tuvid said, the weight of the world hanging in that solitary word.

"No," I snapped at the same time.

Bailey's eyebrows shot up, though she finished the introductions almost lamely. "Tuvid? This is Angie

Granger, owner of Beastly Beer Co. She's had a theft on her property, and she needs our help."

With a growl, I raced around Tuvid's desk and stood in front of him, fists on my hips and my face burning with anger. Gone were my tears—for now. "I don't need help from you."

"Angie." He jumped to his feet, his wings fluttering out to his sides enough to knock a picture off the back wall before he tucked them back close to his spine. "Um, yeah."

I took in all seven feet of him. As a tall—and curvy—woman, I'd adored how tiny I'd felt when I stood beside him in my garden, until he started flinging around wild accusations.

The blue skin on his face darkened, only his closely clipped beard hiding his blush. I'd only briefly dreamed of touching his chiseled jawline, plus his glorious wings pinned to his spine with only the upper, swooping portions topped with spikes jutting above his broad shoulders.

I poked his chest. "This man accused me of theft." I whirled around to face Bailey and Ketar who gaped at us from across the room. "Assign another agent."

"We can't," Bailey said. "Ketar and I are leaving town tomorrow, and we won't be back for a week." She gave Tuvid a weak smile. "We *planned* to leave town, that is."

"I can handle this," Tuvid said in that rumbly voice that for a fraction of a second made my knees melt. Then I stiffened them and fed him another glare. He had the nerve to give me a lazy smile that made my heart thunder and heat coil low in my belly.

"You two go ahead," he added, waving to Katar and Bailey. "I'll take down the information and help Angie."

"Are you alright with that?" Katar asked me, his firm, clipped voice shouting undercover agent.

"You're sure there's no one else available?" I asked, blotting at my eyes with the edge of my sleeve. Where were tissues when I needed them?

"We've got some interviews lined up this week," Katar said. "But for now, Tuvid's my only available agent."

I shoved out a sigh, making my bangs flip up on my forehead before resettling, half of them in my face. I shoved them away. "Alright. We'll make this work."

With a nod and a sharp look thrown Tuvid's way, Katar took Bailey's hand. They backed out of the room, closing the door behind them.

Leaving me alone with *him*.

"Have a seat," he said, waving to the chair on the opposite side of the desk from his. A challenge thrived in his eyes. Yeah, we'd see about that.

I glared, hating that I had no other option than to work with this jerk.

I tried not to notice how he filled out his black t-shirt and his snug jeans. How his wings were a slightly darker blue than the rest of his skin. How I wanted to run my fingertips along the crests of those wings while he shivered and groaned.

I assumed he would. I had no facts to back up that assumption.

"Are your wings erogenous zones?" I blurted out.

His solid brow ridge lifted. "It depends on who's touching them. Sit."

"I'll stand."

"Sit!"

Grumbling, I rounded his desk and dropped into the chair, feeling like a petulant kindergartener called in front of the principal after being caught painting my teacher's doorknob with a glue stick.

Tuvid flashed his fangs, his strong, sharp jawline flexing. For the first time, I found a hint of nervousness in his smile, and that, more than anything, was all it took to deflate my irritation.

"Yes," he said simply.

I blinked. "Yes to what?"

He reached up and tapped one of the spikes on his wings.

I jerked in a breath. "I'm sorry I asked you such a personal question."

"You're curious. I like that." Little crinkles appeared around his eyes when he smiled. They were as steely gray as the stone gargoyles I'd admired while touring Italy, the ones mounted on the tops of the churches. I'd never suspected back then that gargoyles could be real.

I'd never contemplated dating a monster, either, but with one flash of this gargoyle's fangs or one stroke of his fingertips across my face, I worried I'd succumb.

He dropped into his own chair that had slots in the back to accommodate his wings. Back in my garden, and after I'd chewed him out for his unjust accusation, he'd flown away. I'd trotted inside my house and googled gargoyles, pouring over the scant information I found online.

Gargoyles hated having the tips of their wings resting on the ground.

Some mated for life—fated mates, that is.

They were known to lurk on rooftops on occasion.

And every bit of them was as large as the rest. I was stunned to find pictures of their packages, and honestly, I'd stared at them for hours while eating ice cream right out of the container.

I'd had erotic dreams about what this particular gargoyle might do with *his* package if we'd met under different circumstances.

And now I sat across from him, and he was taking my case.

"First, I'd like to apologize for suggesting you stole the gnomes," he said. "I was given the wrong address, and when I spied the ones in your gardens from above, I thought I'd solved the case."

"All you had to do was ask, not accuse me of taking them."

"You're right."

"I am," I said pertly.

His lips quivered.

I couldn't stop mine from doing the same thing.

When I burst into laughter, so did he.

"*I'm* sorry I stormed at you a few moments ago and poked your chest," I said.

"It wasn't much of a poke."

"I'll try harder next time."

"I have a feeling I'd like that as well."

I was vaguely aware of the office door opening and closing again behind me, but I didn't look that way.

"Tell me what you need, Angie," Tuvid said in a growly voice that made me start dreaming of flying in his arms across the starry night sky.

Of stroking his wings.

Of checking out his package.

Get control of yourself, Angie.

"I'm here to . . ." *Think, Angie.* I dragged my gaze away from his, focusing on the papers scattered across his desk. "Someone stole the kegs I planned on entering in the upcoming Monster Mash Brew-off. I need help finding them and I've only got a few days."

"I can do that for you, Angie," he said simply.

My eyes stung.

It was silly, really, but the certainty in his voice was all it took for me to burst into tears.

Get Secret Agent Gargoyle now